The SEAL's Baby
Rogenna Brewer

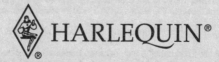

HARLEQUIN®

TORONTO • NEW YORK • LONDON
AMSTERDAM • PARIS • SYDNEY • HAMBURG
STOCKHOLM • ATHENS • TOKYO • MILAN • MADRID
PRAGUE • WARSAW • BUDAPEST • AUCKLAND

ISBN 0-373-71223-5

THE SEAL'S BABY

www.eHarlequin.com

Printed in U.S.A.

For all women who have served their country.

Especially my fellow RomVets loopers—
talented women writers who served in the armed forces.

And my WhatsBrewin and CrewBrew loops—voracious
romance readers who love men and women in uniform.

Books by Rogenna Brewer

HARLEQUIIN SUPERROMANCE

833—SEAL IT WITH A KISS
980—SIGN, SEAL, DELIVER
1070—MIDWAY BETWEEN YOU AND ME

Commander, Helicopter Combat Support
(Special) Squadron Nine
requests the pleasure of your company
at the Change of Command and
Retirement Ceremony

at which
Captain Jon Jordan Loring,
United States Navy
will be relieved by
Lieutenant Commander Hannah C. Stanton,
United States Navy Reserve (Active)

on Friday, the twenty-fifth of July at ten o'clock
Hangar Nine, Naval Air Station North Island
Coronado, California

RSVP   Uniform
(619)545-XXXX   Service Dress Whites

Reception
immediately following the ceremony
Officers' Club, Naval Air Station North Island
Coronado, California

RSVP   Uniform
Card Enclosed   Service Dress Whites

_____

_____

RSVP.
Commander, SEAL Team Eleven
Commander Mike "Mac" McCaffrey,
United States Navy

_____will accept

_____will be unable
to accept the invitation of the
Commander, Helicopter Combat Support
(Special) Squadron Nine
to attend the reception following the Change of
Command and
Retirement Ceremony

CHAPTER ONE

THE ONLY EASY DAY was yesterday. Commander Mike McCaffrey knew the Navy SEAL motto well. He'd just set foot inside Naval Special Warfare Command after five weeks on San Clemente Island, playing bad guy for the BUD/S in training. He still wore woodland-green cammies, complete with war paint, and toted his gear. The thud of heavy boots and raised voices bounced off the walls behind him as Bravo Squad entered to lighten their loads.

"Bravo Eleven, stow it! And blow it!" he called over his shoulder to seven of the best men he'd ever served with.

They knew what he meant. Weekend liberty for the enlisted. Shore leave for the officers. A chance to blow their wads, paycheck or otherwise.

A collective "hoo-yah!" followed the order.

"Hoo-yah," Mike responded, unsure of his own plans for his first duty-free weekend in months. A two-inch thick T-bone ranked at the top of his list. A baked potato with all the fixin's and an ice-cold beer to wash it down. It sure as hell beat endless rations of MRE. Uncle Sam's Meals Ready-to-Eat weren't exactly his idea of home cookin'.

Stopping by the central office to pick up his pigeonholed mail, Mike glanced at the invitation on top. Noting today's date for the Change of Command Ceremony, he was about to deep-six it without even breaking his stride when the relieving officer's name stopped him short.

Hannah.

He backtracked toward the yeoman manning the duty desk. "When did this come in?"

"Sir?" The yeoman looked up. "A couple weeks ago, I think."

"Do I have any messages from a Lieutenant Commander Stanton?" He kept it formal even though any pretense of formality had been stripped once he'd gotten her naked.

"No, sir." The yeoman shook his head. "The only messages are with your mail. Except for one or two and the dailies—they're all from Commander, Naval Special Warfare."

Mike responded with a curt nod and continued down the hall. When he reached his office, he dumped his gear and shut the door behind him. Tossing the rest of the bundled mail to his desk, he held on to the invitation. A quick check of his watch told him what he already knew, he was at least a week too late to RSVP, not to mention the fact that the proceedings had started ten minutes ago. And these things always started on time.

If the Seahawk had picked them up as scheduled he might have made it. Hell, he could have swum the sixty-eight nautical miles in the time they'd spent waiting for the bird this morning.

But it wasn't Mac-Ass-Saving Time. He couldn't turn the clock back one hour let alone one year. If he could there'd be a lot of things he'd change about the past, but Hannah wouldn't be one of them—except maybe he'd savor the moment a little longer.

Twisting his watchband, he wondered if it had been her intention to shackle him with a constant reminder when she'd sent him the damn thing.

Forget?

How could he when her last words to him played like the persistent rattle of urgent Intel coming over his headset? *No regrets, McCaffrey.*

He tossed the invitation to the trash before he conjured up images of soft curves and satin sheets to go along with the voices in his head. As he rounded his desk he dug out the invitation again. He didn't know what to make of it.

Reservists were being called to active duty by the shipload. Hell, he'd spent the better part of the past twelve months in parts unknown, or at least unspoken. Doing the unspeakable. The Teams were recruiting young blood in record numbers and calling up reserve forces. Activated civilian-sailors were being deployed right along with regular Sea, Air and

Land Special Ops. The same would be true for the Wings.

But Hannah? Commander, Helicopter Combat Support (Special) Squadron Nine?

Emphasis on Special Warfare.

A part of him, a very selfish part, was almost glad.

She'd be activated a year or two at least. Which meant they'd be working together, not just training together two weeks a year in the Nevada desert.

Of course that complicated matters. Because the smartest thing she'd ever done was kiss him goodbye.

He shuffled through the rest of his mail and messages while his brain tried to sort out the situation and put it in perspective. She'd be here. They'd be working together. Period.

Too bad that set his pulse into overdrive.

Testing the limits of his self-control, he slammed on the brakes by putting the emphasis back on work. He sat down at his desk, rolled his shoulder to ease the damage done by sleeping on the cold, hard ground, then turned his energies to putting Hannah out of his head.

While processing his mail, he stalled at a message from HCS-9. Had Hannah called after all? That was one possibility. Though in all likelihood, Loring, or someone from Loring's office, had decided to follow up on the invitation. But Mike had Hannah on the brain and his mind held on to that one possibility.

He looked up from the slip of paper to stare at his Choker Whites still in the dry-cleaning bag hanging on the back of his office door. If he were looking for a sign, his Service Dress Whites would be it. Normally the uniform hung in the back of his closet, worn only on those rare occasions when he dressed to impress.

But he wasn't looking for a sign.

Was he?

Shaking free of the notion, he reached for the routing envelope containing the daily SOPA messages and got back to work. The Senior Officer Present Afloat coordinated information among the tenant ship and shore commands in and around the San Diego area. The top message read:

CAPT JJ LORING, USN, WILL BE RELIEVED AS COMMANDER, HCS-9 BY LCDR HC STANTON, USNR, IN CHANGE OF COMMAND/RETIREMENT CEREMONIES 1000 25 JUL AT HANGAR 9 NASNI. ALL INTERESTED PERSONNEL AND THEIR SPOUSES ARE CORDIALLY INVITED TO ATTEND. UNIFORM FOR ATTENDEES IS AS FOLLOWS: SERVICE DRESS WHITES. REQ SOPA ADMIN PASS TO ALL SHIP AND SHORE ACTIVITIES SAN DIEGO AREA.

The Commander, Naval Special Warfare Command had attached a hand written Post-it. *"I'll save you a seat."*

While not a direct order, one was implied—a sign Mike couldn't ignore.

"Ah, hell." He scrubbed a hand over his stubbled, grease-painted kisser. He'd just run out of excuses. Or found the excuse he was looking for.

There'd be no easy out. And no easy day. At least not today. Because today he'd come face-to-face with the woman he'd spent the past three hundred and sixty-five yesterdays trying to forget.

NAVAL AIR STATION NORTH ISLAND
Coronado, California

FROM THE BACK SEAT of her staff car, idling in a line of staff cars, Lieutenant Commander Hannah C. Stanton peeled back a white glove to check her watch. Resigned to her fate, she braced herself with a sigh. These things never started on time, or at least it seemed that way.

In the distance a gull soared above the fleet of gray ladies harbored in San Diego Bay. Following its flight out to sea, Hannah's gaze drifted in the general direction of San Clemente Island. Once again, she found herself fiddling with the band of her Chase-Durer. She'd indulged after receiving orders to active duty. The jeweler's Special Forces collection had prompted her to buy another as a gift.

Impulse control was not her strong suit. At least not when it came to jewelry stores and a certain SPECWAR Operator. But with a little luck and a lot of help from the helicopter pilots over at HCS-5, McCaffrey would be a no-show and the case of B. Stefanouris ouzo it cost her would be worth it.

Even though Commander, SEAL Team Eleven hadn't bothered to RSVP, she couldn't take the chance he'd come. He had a habit of being in the wrong place at the wrong time. Today's Change of Command Ceremony qualified as both. And if anyone knew two wrongs didn't make a right, she did.

Banishing McCaffrey from her mind almost as quickly as he'd vanished from her bed, she sat back and tried to relax. An impossible task with the Navy's *Social Usage And Protocol Handbook* on the seat beside her. She'd read it cover to cover half a dozen times. For every rule there was an exception. For every exception there was an exception.

In this case *she* was the exception, a female commander in the male-dominated world of SPECWAR. One misstep and she'd embarrass her entire sex, not to mention her new command. All eyes were on her, waiting for her to stumble, if not flat out fall.

She shuddered as cold air blasted her from the vent. Despite the chill, her palms were sweating through her gloves. The enormity of the situation made her long for civilian life. She had to keep reminding herself she'd trained for this. Well, not *this*.

She'd trained to fly Seahawks, the Navy's version of the Hawk Class helicopter, for Combat Search and Rescue and Special Warfare Combat Support. But CSAR and SPECWAR ops were a far cry from all this pomp and circumstance. Further still from her safe little niche in the civilian world. Of course how safe would she feel ignoring the danger to her country? She'd much rather be on the front lines doing her duty, and doing it well enough to bring one more soldier or sailor home.

The driver inched the car forward, then stopped. The door opened. The waiting officer offered his free arm while keeping his sword to his side with the other. She accepted with the lightest touch.

Primly keeping her knees together, she swung her legs around and stepped white heels to the curb in a ladylike gesture that did her mother and the Navy proud.

Almost.

"I can take it from here, Spence." She dismissed her dashing co-pilot.

"Sure thing." The younger man winked in understanding as he took a step back.

Billy Idol lyrics in her head, she looked over her own *White Wedding*—or the closest she'd ever come to the real thing—and hoped she wasn't committing career suicide. "Calypso, what have you done?"

She'd been tagged Calypso—after the sea nymph—while still flying CH-46 Sea Knights off the aircraft carrier USS *Enterprise*. On her first SAR mission she'd saved half a dozen stranded Greek fishermen from their sinking boat. Despite the increasing risk from hazardous weather conditions she'd hoisted every last man and the ship's mutt aboard the helicopter. The grateful sailors had toasted her with a bottle of ouzo they'd salvaged from the wreckage, convinced only one of the Titan's own could have pulled off the stunt.

They didn't know how right they were.

At least Calypso had forever replaced Bubbles, the name a less-than-PC instructor had cursed her with in flight school. She hated that it made her sound like a stripper. But more than that she hated that it called attention to her weakest area in training—water.

One panic attack while upside down in the Dilbert Dunker, and she'd become infamous for those tiny little oxygen bubbles that rose to the surface when she hadn't. Worse than almost drowning, worse than Navy swimmers having to rescue her from the simulated cockpit, was having to do it all over again or wash out of the program.

She'd made it out of the harness and to the surface on her second go-round and every time since when she updated her quals. But not without that feeling of utter panic.

That dunk tank was easy compared to this.

She took a last deep breath before taking her next career plunge.

Assuming command was very much like a marriage. It required commitment and, in this case, compromise. The only thing missing was her bouquet. And, of course, there was no groom caught in the crosshairs of her sights.

And no father of the bride at her side.

Hannah stepped onto the white carpet. Alone.

So much for embarrassing missteps. She'd now committed a major faux pas. With deliberate pride.

Pride goeth before the fall. So you damn well better not trip all over it, Stanton.

A pair of side boys, the appropriate honors for a lieutenant commander, stood at attention. On the Executive Officer's command they rendered sharp hand salutes. Two gongs sounded. Then the XO, as Master of Ceremonies, announced her arrival.

The handbook said single ladies were to be escorted, but single female officers fell into a gray area. Because nowhere in that book did it say single male officers had to be escorted down the aisle.

First impressions were important. In marriage as in life, one should start out as one intended to go along. For Hannah that meant going without leaning on any man.

One last gong followed her march through the white-topped VIP tent. Despite her bravado, she missed her father more than she had since that day two Naval officers had shown up at their door. She would have liked to hear him say he was proud of her today.

Climbing the steps to the red-white-and-blue-swagged dais, she reached her seat to the left of Captain Loring. Admiral Riker, the highest-ranking official taking part in the ceremony, sat to Loring's right. The chaplain sat to her left and the XO stood at a podium to the far right. The podium in the center remained open for their use.

"All rise for the national anthem," the XO requested.

As she rendered honors to the flag, Hannah got her first good look at the assembled crowd. The squadron stood by in formation. The guests got to their feet from uniform rows of folding chairs. Except for a white rose, the first chair to the left of the aisle remained empty, in memory of Captain Loring's deceased wife. The second chair held the folded triangle that had adorned the casket of Hannah's father. Her mother, Rosemary Stanton, pressed a kiss to the bud she held and placed it on the flag beside her before covering her heart with her hand.

After that, everything became a blur set to band music as Hannah blinked back tears. Sometimes sacrifices were made on the battlefield. But just as often they were made on the home front.

Her younger sister Sammy, bouncing baby in her arms, stood beside their mother. The three-month-old needing all the attention was Hannah's own precious daughter.

Fortunately her mother and sister were willing to go above and beyond the call of duty. If Sammy hadn't been able to move to California, Hannah as a single mom would have been forced to leave her daughter behind with her family in Colorado.

Adventure aside, the United States Navy was a job 24/7.

She had to be deployable.

No excuses. Not even little ones. Like wanting to spend time with her baby girl.

Or big ones. Like wanting to keep her daughter from knowing the pain of losing a parent.

"The Star Spangled Banner" ended, and the XO requested everyone remain standing for the Chaplain's invocation.

Hannah mouthed the words *thank you* to her mother and sister.

She had a two-year obligation to Uncle Sam and the two hundred men and women of HCS-9. In answering the call to duty she'd given up more than family time and social ties, more than a mid-six-figure salary in the aerospace industry and a plot of real estate in the Rocky Mountains. She'd given up her peace of mind. Because sooner or later she'd run into McCaffrey and out of excuses.

When she did, she'd need her family more than ever.

They'd been there for her when he hadn't.

Seated once again, her gaze shifted to the audience. She tried hard not to make the comparison between the empty chair reserved for her father and the empty chair among the SEAL commanders. McCaffrey wasn't here, but he'd been safe and sound when the Fire Hawks of HCS-5 picked him up from San Clemente Island. And as long as he stayed away so was their daughter.

The baby slept through most of the speeches, but

woke fussy. Already showing signs of independence, like her mother, a chubby fist found its way to a rosebud mouth in the time it took Auntie Sammy to dig through the diaper bag for a bottle. Hannah somehow managed to maintain her military bearing even as every maternal instinct she possessed made her want to leap from the platform. But her complement of uniforms didn't include Wonder Woman or Super Mom costumes, just a flight suit and the wings of a Naval Special Warfare Aviator.

Captain Loring stepped center stage, the cue for the participants on the dais to stand once again.

"The Change of Command Ceremony is a Navy tradition without equal in the Army or Air Force," he began. "Custom has established that this observance be both formal and impressive while at its heart is the reading of official orders." After a lengthy speech, he got around to doing just that. Afterward he turned to Hannah. "Ma'am, I am ready to be relieved."

Hannah stepped forward and read her orders. As courtesy demanded of the relieving officer, she kept her comments brief. When finished, she turned to Loring and executed a sharp salute. "I relieve you, sir."

Captain Loring returned the salute. "I stand relieved."

The Color Guard marched forward. Loring ordered his command pennant lowered, followed by Hannah ordering hers broken, readying it for unfurling. On command, the Color Guard raised her banner. Wind snapped it to attention. Above the command flag for the North Island Night Hawks of HCS-9, the simple white pennant bearing the silver eagle of a captain had been replaced by the silver oak leaf of a lieutenant commander.

Hannah turned to salute her immediate superior in the Chain of Command—Admiral Riker, Commander, Helicopter Wing Reserve. "Lieutenant Commander Hannah C. Stanton reporting for duty, sir."

CHAPTER TWO

WITH ALL THE FORMALITIES OVER, except the receiving line, the squadron had been dismissed to "mill about smartly." Which meant they were to remain on their toes. The Navy band played an endless stream of John Philip Sousa compositions. Officer and enlisted mingled under the shade of the open hangar bay and the scattered trees near the grassy knoll that separated the blacktop grinder from the paved parking lot. Distinguished military and civilian guests filed out from under the tent to pass through the line.

As protocol demanded, Hannah exchanged more white-gloved salutes and handshakes. To her left stood the departing CO. To her right the XO, because the book said a proper receiving line should not end with a lady, and the lady in question had no hand in the planning of today's events. Otherwise she would have seen to that detail, as well.

"Congratulations, Commander Stanton."

"Thank you for coming, Admiral Moore." The exchange with the Commanding Officer of North Island lasted only as long as their brief hand clasp.

Since he was also the Commanding Officer, Naval
Base Coronado, Naval Amphibious Base Coronado,
Outlying Field Imperial Beach, Navy Radio Receiving Facility, Mountain Training Facility LaPosta,
Warner Springs Training Area and Naval Air Landing Facility San Clemente Island, that pretty much
made him the most important man present.

Whether he supported her in her new roll as the CO
of HCS-9 remained to be seen. She did note, however,
that he'd dropped "Lieutenant" from her rank, but
whether that was out of courtesy for her new title or
simply Navy shorthand she didn't know. At least she'd
chalked up eight titles with one handshake. How many
more to go before the good ol' boys actually accepted
her as one of them? Like that would ever happen.

Over the departing admiral's gleaming gold
shoulder board, she spotted a charter member of the
boy's club—one of the *Bad Boys of Bravo*. The
Commander of SEAL Team Eleven, Mike "Mac"
McCaffrey. He climbed out of his rust-bucket Jeep
Wrangler, looking for all the world as if he'd staged
his late arrival. Mirrored sunglasses in place, he
reached back into the open cab for his headgear, then
disappeared in a sea of white.

Hannah almost missed her cue to address the next
uniform in line. Recovering with a sharp salute, she
once again extended her white-gloved hand and exchanged a few polite words with Commander, Naval
Special Warfare, Rear Admiral Warren Bell and his
wife, Lucy.

"Call me Lu." The woman's exotic eyes suggested various ports of call where the couple might have met. A romantic notion at best. Mrs. Bell spoke English with the accent of a native Southern Californian. "Let's skip the formality of a social call, Commander—may I call you Hannah?—and do lunch. Just us girls." She glanced toward her husband. "Warren won't mind, will you, dear?"

Lu's question seemed perfunctory at best.

Admiral Bell shrugged. "I can see it's out of my hands. However, I did wish to speak with the Commander—"

"Libby doesn't need her father running interference, Warren."

"Petty Officer Bell is your daughter? I'm sorry I hadn't made the connection." Hannah had committed the squadron roster to memory, including the detachment of rescue swimmers. "You must be very proud. Only a handful of women have ever made the cut."

"The same could be said for Seahawk pilots."

Hannah acknowledged the admiral's compliment with a nod. At least she took it as a compliment. To even qualify she'd had to log over two thousand hours in the cockpit, and a command position was a long shot even for a man. "Is there a problem with Libby?"

"Absolutely not," Lu said.

"We'll discuss it later," was the admiral's noncommittal dismissal.

The remaining parade of names and faces passed by in a forgettable haze. Hannah told herself she'd only imagined McCaffrey because he was the last man on earth she wanted to see right now.

The receiving line had trickled down to one last handshake when the hairs on the back of her neck stood on end. She didn't need to turn around to know *he* stood right behind her. Her radar had been fine-tuned to Mac years ago. As the others in line drifted away in private conversation, she dared to turn around.

McCaffrey leaned against the now-empty grandstand. His broader shoulders and badder attitude set him apart from the rest. If it wasn't for the Ray-Ban Predators he hooked to his breast pocket, the attitude might have been subdued by his Choker Whites. He pushed away from the platform and strode toward her.

Taking a deep breath, she sucked in her stomach. Twelve weeks of no carbs and brutal crunches still hadn't primed her for this moment. Why did he have to look so damn ready for heart-stopping action in that uniform?

Her fingers twitched as she prepared to salute the rank of commander he wore on his epaulets. Just as she was about to execute the move, he outmaneuvered her by removing his cover. Hat in hand, looking anything but humble, he stopped a few paces from her. Dark crew-cut hair. Dark, unreadable eyes.

His gesture might have escaped notice in the gaslamp district of San Diego. But the Navy had its traditions. Written and unwritten. He may as well have announced to everyone present they'd slept together.

Heat scalded her cheeks. Even legendary sea nymphs were entitled to one mistake with a sailor. Unfortunately, most of those epic stories ended in tragedy. This one was no different. Not that making love to Mike McCaffrey could ever be considered a tragedy. But falling in love with him might…

And committing to *his and hers* towels would mean hanging her career out to dry. Not to mention her heart. And her daughter's.

McCaffrey surveyed her curves with the precision of a mine sweep. For once she could read exactly what was on his mind. He'd been hunkered down with his men for weeks on end during war games on San Clemente Island. He was male. He was horny. And that was pure unadulterated lust in his eyes.

"You look good, Han."

"Don't—" She crossed her arms, straining her uniform jacket, which had already been let out two inches in the bustline. "Don't you dare—"

"Careful, Commander," he warned. "Finish that sentence and I might think you actually missed me."

She bit back her natural inclination to deny missing him. Why give the guy more ammo when he already carried a full clip? He was right about one thing—in a crowd of no less than six flag officers, she needed to be careful.

When she didn't parry his remark, his jaw tensed, drawing attention to the spot of tissue just below his ear. She hated to think bureaucratic decisions made the Teams easy targets, but SEALs had been ordered to shave nonregulation beards grown in an effort to blend in with Middle Eastern customs. Shortly afterward Mac had been shot protecting a new and fragile democracy. She'd gleaned that bit of information from CNN. His shoulder bore the scar of that decision and must hurt like the devil when he abused it. And she knew he abused it.

She wanted to reach out, brush away the blood-spotted tissue and let her hand linger along the hard line of his jaw, trace his firm lips with the pad of her thumb, and that was just for starters. She wanted to kiss every inch of him, every scar, old and new—if she didn't scratch out his eyes first.

"One of us was in a hurry to get here," she said.

He ignored the gibe and followed her gaze with a curious hand beneath his ear. "Rush job," he admitted, sweeping away the evidence. He broke eye contact in that instant, but only for a second. "I didn't miss you either, Han."

Her heart did stop then and it had nothing to do with his uniform. It would be safer to stay angry at him than to look for hidden meaning behind his words. Otherwise she risked opening a floodgate of emotions.

"You have lousy timing, McCaffrey."

Really…lousy…timing.

Where were you a year ago? Three months? Yesterday?

Of course she knew. A year ago he'd been sent to the Middle East—though who knew where else after that. Three months ago he'd returned to the States, and yesterday he'd been a few miles away on San Clemente Island.

Today he stood right in front of her, a lifetime too late for everything she'd wanted to say to him. And everything she wanted him to say to her.

As Calypso she had full access to a part of his life he'd otherwise never be able to share. Next time he put his life on the line she'd be there to cover his six. And she'd do it again and again. Because of that there was one line they could never cross again.

"So you have nothing to say for yourself?" she asked.

Mike scanned the thinning crowd. The band played a Sousa trumpet-and-drum piece, "Hannah, My True Love." His eyes returned to her, just as he knew he would. She looked uptight, prim and proper, not like Hannah at all—except maybe the dangerous curves restrained by tailored Dress Whites. He'd only seen her in a skirt once before. But he didn't need a visual of her silk-clad legs to imagine them wrapped around him. "I think my timing is just about perfect."

"To embarrass me?"

"Nobody noticed. And if they did, they don't care. It's acceptable for an officer to remove his cover outdoors in a social situation. Especially in the presence of a lady."

"Bite your tongue. And you're no gentleman, either."

"You just figured that out?"

"I've had a year to mull it over."

"I don't rate more than a few minutes of mulling." He searched her eyes for some sign that she'd thought about him for more than sixty seconds after he'd gone but resigned himself to the truth. "Not even that."

"Not even that," she agreed.

Standing this close, he could see beyond the flare of her temper to the hurt in her green eyes. She may not have given him a second thought, but the first one had been enough to piss her off.

Short, wispy curls framed her flushed face. When he'd left, her hair had been around her shoulders. But a lot more than her appearance had changed. "What happened to 'no regrets'?"

He followed those expressive eyes to his wrist and lifted his sleeve a fraction to satisfy her curiosity.

"You're wearing it?" She sounded surprised.

"Why wouldn't I? Chronograph functions down to the tenth of a second. Advanced illumination system. Even an underwater resistance rating up to three hundred and thirty feet. What more could a Navy SEAL want?" He didn't even try to hide the bite of sarcasm.

"Nothing, I'm sure."

Nothing? Not when everything he wanted stood right in front of him. And just out of reach.

"You can't wear it in the field."

"I kept my go-to-hell watch." Navy issue. No personal information, nothing that could be traced back to Uncle Sam. Which gave his Uncle deniability if he were ever captured someplace where the U.S. had no business being. Unlike the Chase-Durer, which was not only traceable, but contained enough personal information to make him vulnerable to the enemy. If only he knew what that personal information meant. He unfastened the security clasp and read the inscription on the back, "*No regrets. Fallon.* If my memory is correct it was Reno, not Fallon, Nevada. How about a decoder ring to go along with it?"

When women started giving him gifts he knew it was past time to cut bait and run. But the gifts were usually more cute 'n' cuddly. And every guy knew that after the stuffed animals came the kittens and the puppies and the expectations of a long-term commitment.

He and Hannah had had one night.

No expectations. No commitment.

Just sex. Mind-blowing, falling-off-the-bed-and-onto-the-floor sex. All-night-long-and-into-the-next-morning sex. Couldn't-get-enough-of-each-other sex. Sex and something more they'd never be able to explore because it had been preempted by his pager.

"So is the watch a memento? Or an expensive kiss-off?"

"I have good taste," she said. "Your point?"

His hand closed over the watch face. What was she telling him? "It brought me this far."

"I'm going to have to borrow that decoder ring."

"Aren't we both just holding out to see which of us can hold out the longest?"

"Is that the game we're playing?"

She shifted in those sexy-as-hell heels, making her better equipped for interrogation than any enemy. He was spilling his guts here, but she wasn't giving him any quarter. "You should have called or written, McCaffrey."

"That works both ways."

Her mouth opened, then closed again as if she'd been about to say something and thought better of it. He could imagine the tongue-lashing she wanted to deliver. The morning-after felt awkward enough without it taking place a year later. He'd just never thought it would be this awkward with Hannah. She knew who and what he was. Because they were two of a kind. If it hadn't been his pager, it would have been hers.

"I'm sorry if you have regrets, Han, but I don't."

"What did you expect?" she asked with a defiant tilt to her chin. "Open arms?"

Something like that.

Maybe not.

Which was why he hadn't made the connection when he picked up the phone in Manila, P.I. Or Bagram Air Base, Afghanistan. Or Coronado, California. What could he say?

They'd both changed. For her, life had gone on. For him, it had been put on hold. He remembered every detail of their night together as if it were yesterday, which didn't mean he could just pick up where he'd left off. Where *they'd* left off.

Time had created an unbreachable distance.

"You arranged the late bird this morning," he said with resignation. "If you didn't want me here, why the invite?"

"I didn't invite you. In fact I tried to *uninvite* you, but you're a hard man to track down."

"I see." He compressed his lips. That solved the mystery of the phone call.

Pity shone in her eyes. "You don't see at all."

But he knew a see-you-around-sucker when he heard one. Not that that was possible. Every time his team needed a ride she'd be there. He held her gaze until she dropped his.

"See you around, Han." He'd be damned if he'd let her say it first. He'd already set aside his pride to come here today. He had nothing left to give. Shoving the watch into his pocket, he turned his back on her and everything they might have had together. Who was he kidding, they'd never had a chance.

"Mike, wait! Please…"

His hands stilled in the automatic action of putting on his cover and he brought it back down to his side. Turning back around, he wished his heart hadn't taken that leap when she'd called his name. Because right now it was stuck somewhere in his throat.

"You didn't make me any promises you didn't keep. Let's just leave it at that, okay?"

Her admission wasn't much of a consolation

prize. But he offered a curt nod. "For what it's worth, I know I blew it."

Her eyes softened to the color of moss after a midday shower in the jungles of the P.I. He knew because he'd spent six months of the past year making that direct comparison. It beat the hell out of counting bloodthirsty mosquitoes taking bites out of his thick hide.

For the first time since he'd approached her, she let her guard down and uncrossed her arms. "Mike, there's something—"

Whatever Hannah had been about to say she kept to herself. Checking over his shoulder, he discovered an older woman had intruded on their moment. Midfifties. Trim figure. Designer pantsuit, all white. Salon-enhanced red hair.

Hannah's mother?

The approaching woman clung to a tri-folded flag. No red showed, in reverence to the blood shed. Mike had seen more than enough of that symbol in the past few months to last a lifetime. He wouldn't be standing here in this awkward silence if his Choker Whites hadn't been stained by a young widow's tears three months ago.

Hannah had never mentioned having a father who'd died in service to his country. Come to think of it, Hannah had never mentioned a father. Or a family. He knew every curve of her body, but he didn't really know her at all.

"Hannah," the woman called out, "they're waiting for you over at the Officers' Club."

"Be right there, Mother. Just give me a moment—"

But Hannah's mother wasn't about to be dismissed that easily. She drew even with him and smiled. "You're welcome to join us, Commander," she correctly identified him by rank. "Is that a Navy SEAL Trident…" Her gaze swept over his budwiser and the ribbons on his chest that proved he led his team from the front lines and not behind a desk. Which was the only reason he could face those widows at all. Her smile faded as she settled on his name tag. "Commander McCaffrey?"

"*The* Mike McCaffrey? Navy SEAL extraordinaire?" The query came from a younger woman. Shorter, chubbier, more blond than redheaded and pushing a baby stroller. "Commander of SEAL Team Eleven? The team that drills with my sister's squadron every year in Fallon, Nevada? The same Mike McCaffrey who drove my sister to the airport in Reno last summer—"

"Enough, Sam." Hannah cut her off with a look. Mike didn't know what that look meant. Only that he didn't want to be on the receiving end of it.

The sister turned wide green eyes on Hannah. A Stanton trademark if he wasn't mistaken.

"I see my reputation precedes me." He raised an eyebrow in question. He'd driven Hannah to the airport, but she'd been bumped from the flight. From there they'd checked into a hotel suite and gambled with their friendship—a lose/lose proposition at best.

One he couldn't regret. But whatever her family thought they knew about him, it wasn't good.

"All bad," Hannah assured him.

No doubt.

He felt an urgent need to break the ice with a better first impression. "How about introductions?" he insisted, tucking his cover under his arm.

True to form, Hannah gave in to his request with the grace of good manners. "Commander…my mother, Rosemary Stanton."

"Ma'am." He extended his hand.

Her mother didn't.

"Samantha, Hannah's sister," the sister latched on to his hand, "her younger, recently single sister. Should I call you Mac or Mike, Commander?" She pumped his arm as she pumped him for information, but it would have been hard not to notice the mother's cool reception. The simple fact that they even knew his name should have told him something. He'd hurt Hannah. Of course he'd chosen that route as being the least complicated.

"It's Mac." He smiled anyway. "Mike gets confusing in the field."

"Mike is the phonetic letter *M*," Hannah offered the explanation.

He had his own. She'd called out Mike, not Mac or McCaffrey when he'd come inside her, and she'd called out Mike just a few minutes ago.

"So, Mac," the sister said, "are there any more like you at home?"

"As you can see, I'm one of a kind." He managed to extract his hand while evading her real question. He had a brother. Not to mention four sisters.

Hannah's sister assessed him with the same openness as in her demeanor. She had a pretty face and generous curves beneath a gauzy summer dress. She also had a kid and no wedding band. She'd said she was recently single.

Divorced? Widowed? In his experience widows wore their rings a lot longer than *recently*. But anything was possible. The flag her mother carried could belong to her. Samantha Stanton seemed to expect something from him, and it wasn't his shoulder.

He glanced at the stroller. The sleeping rug rat squirmed, scrunching its face until it turned cherry red. He recognized that look thanks to his half-dozen nieces and nephews, glad that was one diaper he didn't have to change. Three of his four sisters were married, two with kids. The youngest, Meg was still single. So was their brother, Buddy. But while they all shared the same gene pool, Buddy had that something extra that made him special.

Of course, every mother thought her kid was special. "Cute kid." It was the right thing to say.

Samantha Stanton beamed at him. "Do you like children, Commander?"

"Mac," he reminded her. "Sure." He shrugged. "As long as they're somebody else's."

CHAPTER THREE

"EXCUSE ME, I have a cake to cut." Hannah left Mc-Caffrey and her family, but especially Mac, to make of her exit what they would. She had to get away before she did or said something she might regret.

He liked kids as long as they're *somebody else's.* What else had she expected?

"Hannah! Hannah, wait up." Sammy pushed the stroller at a slight jog to keep up with Hannah's military stride. "He didn't mean anything by it. He thinks—"

Hannah stopped short, turning on her sister. "I know what he thinks, Sam. Excuse me, *Samantha,*" she corrected.

"Excuse me?"

"Oh, come on, Sammy, you've never gone by Samantha a day in your life! What's with you? Flirting with Fallon's father. Pretending to be her mother—"

"I never did any of that. He just assumed."

Hannah took a deep breath, deep enough for the flush of anger and jealousy to fade just a little. She was only picking a fight with her sister because she wanted to go fifteen rounds with Mac.

"I know, I'm sorry." Hannah glanced toward Mc-Caffrey, who was still talking to her mother. His assumptions played into Hannah's deepest fears—that in the end it would be Sammy raising their daughter. "Have I told you today how much I love and appreciate you?"

"Don't go getting all mushy on me now."

"I know I don't say it often enough."

"Forget it," Sammy said. "I know you're upset. And I didn't help any by playing devil's advocate."

"You're not the only one." Hannah nodded toward their mother. A few minutes ago she'd snubbed McCaffrey, now they were engaged in animated conversation. "What in the world do you suppose they have to talk about?"

"The weather?"

"Funny."

"Don't worry. Your secret's safe," Sammy said with real regret. "You and Mom are cut from the same cloth. Neither of you would ever air your dirty laundry in public."

Hannah returned her full attention to her sister. "What's that supposed to mean?"

"It means Mom's going to keep mum. I think she invented the term *soldier on.* And you…I don't know why you ever left active duty for the reserves in the first place. The uniform suits you. You button up all your emotions inside that white jacket, and they reward you for it with those ribbons worn in place of your heart."

"I'm not emotionless," Hannah denied. "I just keep my feelings to myself. Do you honestly think I don't feel anything?"

"Then you deserve a Purple Heart. Because if you're bleeding, nobody knows it. Least of all him."

"It doesn't matter. McCaffrey means nothing to me. *Less than nothing,*" she emphasized. "A one-night stand with a military man. How much more cliché can it get?"

Although, technically, she'd known him for more than one night. Well enough to know he didn't want children. Just the same it hurt to hear him say it out loud.

"Nothing?" her sister asked over the stroller she rocked back and forth.

Hannah stole a glance at her daughter. She'd dressed Fallon in a cute pink sailor dress and hat for the festivities. Her eyes were still shut tight. Otherwise McCaffrey would have seen how much they looked like his own. "Okay, so maybe he meant something to me once. But from now on he's just the sperm donor."

"You have to tell him. If you've been waiting for the right opportunity—"

"That opportunity has long since passed. It would be different if I were still a civilian. But no good can come from telling him now. Or anyone else for that matter."

This was another one of those gray areas.

She'd be better off letting her military co-workers believe, as most of her civilian co-workers did, that she was a thirty-three-year-old woman tired of waiting for Mr. Right, so she'd decided to have a baby on her own. Somehow it seemed more acceptable than the truth.

She'd made a mistake. She'd taken responsibility. She didn't need McCaffrey to do his duty. Because the truth was she *was* a thirty-three-year-old woman who'd given up on finding Mr. Right a long time ago. Which didn't mean she was going to settle for Commander Wrong.

If McCaffrey had thought enough of her and their one night together to keep in touch, maybe they would have had a chance to work something out.

That works both ways. His challenge echoed.

She'd started so many letters during her pregnancy, all crumpled after a line or two. Aside from being at a loss for words, she could admit that stubborn pride had kept her from finishing even a single note. She'd wanted him to make the first move.

He'd made his move today.

After an invitation he'd thought she'd sent.

And long after she'd sent him the watch. She now regretted that impulse. In a moment of weakness, she'd dropped the watch into the mailbox. She'd been at the post office mailing Fallon's birth announcements. The announcement she intended for him never made it into the box. But the clues were there if, and that was a big if, he chose to decipher them. Then what?

"Even sperm donors have some say in the matter," Sammy said with such a look of pity Hannah had to wonder how long she'd been lost in her own thoughts.

"I can't deal with this right now. Fallon needs changing. And I need to get over to the O Club where I'm sure an impatient photographer is waiting."

"I'll change Fallon," Sammy offered.

"I've got her. I'll just be a minute." Hannah picked up the reassuring weight of her daughter. Wrestling the stroller single-handed, she headed toward her office inside Hangar Nine. "He didn't mean it," she whispered with her cheek pressed against the baby's, although she wasn't quite sure which one of them needed reassuring. She felt an ache in her breast that had nothing to do with her milk letting down.

Fallon rooted for a nipple, settling on those ribbons above Hannah's heart. Putting on the uniform did make Hannah feel different. But honor, courage and commitment to the core values of the Navy didn't make her heartless or mean she had anything less to give her daughter. In many ways it meant she was willing to give her daughter more.

"Enough now. Auntie Sammy already fed you."

After Fallon had been born, Hannah had considered contacting McCaffrey through third-party notification. His command, her command, even his family would have been able to send him a Health and Welfare message through the American Red Cross. But did she really want him hearing that he was a father through a SOPA?

Chances were, as CO, he'd have seen the message even before the chaplain had a chance to soften the blow. What would his reaction have been? What if he'd been in a hot zone? Would he have been able to do his duty without distraction? Would he have even got the message?

There were too many unknown variables. With time they'd turned into obstacles.

Pride wasn't the only thing that had kept her from tracking him down. Doubts about his desire to be a father had crept in. The fact that she knew he'd do his duty regardless only hurt her more. And then Fallon had been born, and Hannah felt the overwhelming need to protect her daughter. Fallon didn't need a father who'd be in and out of her life so often he'd cease to exist even in her memories.

The single cloudy memory Hannah had of her own father was of him leaving. Her daughter deserved more.

Just as she reached the door to her office, the cell phone in the diaper bag started ringing. Hannah propped the door open with the stroller and grabbed for the phone.

She picked up at the same time she settled Fallon on the couch in her office. "Hello?" She sat down angled toward her daughter and continued to dig in the bag for the necessary diaper and wipes.

"Hannah, it's Peter."

"Is everything all right?"

"You mean aside from the fact this project is falling apart without you? We need you, Hannah. I need you."

"You don't need me, Peter. You only think you do."

"I'm a rocket scientist, not a manager. You know I don't know which way is up without you."

"You'll do fine. You have good people working for you—"

"I lost my glasses yesterday. And today I lost my spare."

"Look up…on top of your head."

He clicked his tongue, apparently finding them right where she'd said they'd be. "That just proves my point. I need you. Maybe you could fly back for the weekend?"

"Peter—"

"Just for the weekend—"

"I can't. You know I can't."

"I thought you might say that."

She felt annoyed with him for even asking. She'd cut her maternity leave short to minimize the effect of her longer military absence on the company. He didn't understand that, at least temporarily, she was no longer available to him. By law he had to hold her job for her. As a friend there was no question that he would. If there was a company to go back to. With so many reservists deploying, it impacted small businesses and big-city police forces alike. She was Peter's Gal Friday. He counted on her. "If you're that desperate maybe—"

"I've already booked a flight."

"I was going to say, maybe you could e-mail the proposal, and I could find some time to look it over." What was she saying? What time? "Peter—"

"Did you get the flowers?"

Hannah was busy peeling the tabs on the clean diaper she'd managed to wrestle under Fallon's bare bottom, but she wedged the phone between her neck and shoulder and looked around the office. There was a bouquet on her desk. One more wedding item. "Yes."

"And?" he prompted.

"They're beautiful," she said, folding the poopy diaper and stashing it in a plastic bag for later disposal. She'd have to pick up a Diaper Genie for her office. Maybe bring in a portable playpen and some toys… What was she thinking? It wasn't like she'd be bringing Fallon to the office every day or even be here herself. With less than seventy-two hours' notice she could be anywhere in the world. Including the latest hot zone.

"You haven't read the card, have you?"

"No, I'm sorry." She cleaned her hands with a baby wipe. "I've been…busy—"

"I understand."

Did he really?

Her daughter was now clean and content, gurgling in response to Hannah's smiles. Peter's voice barely registered as Hannah got caught up in playing peekaboo.

"Is that Fallon cooing in the background?"

"She's a *Charmin Chatty* with a big *beau-ti-ful* smile," she emphasized for the baby. See for yourself." She snapped and sent the digital image from her camera phone to his. "I'm glad you always manage to talk me into the latest gadgets."

"So am I."

She took several more pictures. During the photo shoot, Fallon surprised them both by rolling over onto her belly with help from the seat cushion. Lifting her bobble head, she peeked over her shoulder looking for Hannah.

"Yes, Mommy sees your new trick." She smiled at her daughter's stunned expression. Fallon's whole face lit up, her arms and legs windmilled, celebrating the joy of her newfound talent. She was already a handful, but she was really going to be a handful when she started crawling. Hannah could only hope she'd be there to see it. "Did you catch all that?" she asked Peter.

"I miss you both," he said.

"We miss you, too."

"How do you feel about long-distance relationships?"

He was a good boss. And a better friend. Perhaps that's why it was so easy for them to take each other for granted. But he was not without his faults. Sometimes she thought he mistook their friendship for something more. Poor Peter. He needed someone the exact opposite of her. Which was why she didn't assign a deeper meaning to his words. But he deserved an answer.

Saved by a knock on her office door.

"Peter, I have to go." She hung up on his goodbye.

The Commander, Naval Special Warfare, poked his bald head around the open door. This was the first time she'd seen him uncovered. The look suited a man of his stature. "Did I catch you at a bad time?"

"No!" She picked up Fallon and stood. "Admiral Bell, come in, please." She gestured toward the couch where she'd just finished changing the baby. He remained standing, which was probably just as well considering he wore white from head to toe.

"We didn't get much time in the receiving line. I just wanted to find out how you were settling in."

"I've only been here a couple of days for orientation, but fine, so far."

"Good, good." He moved farther into the office, picking up the picture of Fallon from Hannah's desk. "Have you enrolled her in swimming lessons yet? They offer Mommy and Me classes on base. I regret not having that experience with Libby. Drown-proofing SEAL style was the extent of our lessons."

Hannah pushed the disturbing image aside. She doubted that meant he'd thrown his daughter into a pool with hands and feet bound like the BUD/S in training. Still… "You must have made up for it at some point. She obviously loves the water now." Hannah wouldn't be drown-proofing her own daughter anytime soon—if ever.

"Almost drowned when she was six. Riptide out in the Bay. For years she wouldn't go near water. But as you pointed out, she loves it now."

"Did you need to speak with me about Libby, Admiral?"

"It's nothing really." He took her cue and set the picture aside. "Just that she doesn't like being the admiral's kid. So…no special treatment, you understand. She wants to find her own way in the world. Which is of course why she enlisted when her mother and I would have preferred she get a college education and a commission. Or steer clear of military service altogether." He hesitated for a moment. "She transferred into your unit, Commander, because she sees you as a role model."

Hannah adjusted Fallon higher on her shoulder.

His wise gaze settled on her and the baby in her arms. "I understand you're a single mother?"

Hannah stiffened. "Yes, sir."

"I imagine you feel a little like you've been thrown in the deep end."

"We're keeping our heads above water."

"I'm assuming you have a parenting plan in place?"

This wasn't the civilian world. He had a right, a responsibility to pry. But men in general just didn't get it. She needed a wife more than she needed a husband.

"Just like every other working mother in America."

"Only the commute is to hell in a helicopter and the business trips last months, even years," he pointed out.

"My note to the nanny includes a power of attorney. And a will. I've filled out the Navy's Dependent Care Certificate. I could fax a copy to your office—" She rummaged the Out box on her desk for proof. "My sister's taken on the baby's guardianship—"

"That won't be necessary, Commander. I'm just checking to see that everything's a go for Monday."

"Yes, of course. Squadron Nine has coordinated efforts for the joint training op with SEAL Team One. We'll be wheels up at 0700 sharp."

"Just the same, if you need anything, *anything at all,* don't hesitate to ask…"

"Thank you, Admiral. I'm indebted—"

He shook his head. "Your father already paid that debt."

Hannah's chest tightened.

"Did you know him?" She failed to keep the wistfulness out of her voice.

"We served together for a time in the brown water Navy of Vietnam. He hated those mud puddles…" The admiral broke off eye contact. "He spoke of you often."

True or not, it was the nicest possible thing he could have said to her. "And after the war?"

The admiral shook his head. "He stayed with Team One. And I went on to form the counterterrorist group, Team Eleven."

"They told my mother he died in a training accident."

He wasn't supposed to die. The war was over. He'd promised to return. He'd kissed her and her sister and her mother and he'd promised.

"What can I bring you for your birthday, pumpkin?"

"An Easy Bake oven."

He looked helplessly at her mother, standing in the doorway, holding the baby. "Are you sure you're old enough? How old are you going to be anyway? Five? Six?" he teased.

"Seven, Daddy. You know I'm going to be seven."

"Seven. You can't be seven. You're growing up too fast." He lifted her in the air and spun her around. "I'm going to have to start beating those boys off with a baseball bat. Are you sure I can't bring you a new ball and glove?"

She giggled. "You can bring me whatever you want, Daddy, as long as you promise you'll be home to help blow out the candles and cut the cake."

He didn't promise in words, he never promised in words. But he hugged her so tight the promise didn't have to be spoken, it was there in the way he loved her.

The admiral didn't comment further. He simply nodded and changed the subject. "If I'm not mistaken, last year around this time your squadron drilled with Team Eleven, McCaffrey and his boys?"

What could she say except "Yes, sir."

Maybe the admiral didn't think the change in subject was such a stretch. He followed his question with a lifted eyebrow, clearly expecting her to elaborate.

She didn't.

He offered one last bit of advice. "Sometimes the only way to conquer a fear is to face the harsh reality of it."

When he left, Hannah breathed a sigh of relief. She strapped Fallon back into her stroller, then quickly stripped out of her uniform jacket. She'd soaked through her nursing pads to her blouse.

Luckily she kept spare uniforms at the office and still had a few of her dwindling supply of nursing pads in the diaper bag. Monday would be her first separation from her baby girl—two weeks of training exercises in the Nevada desert. Weaning Fallon earlier than she would have liked had been one of those not so small sacrifices required to do her job.

Buttoning her jacket after changing blouses, she decided to bolster her confidence with an old flight-school trick. She picked up an orange, an apple and a stress ball from her desk. "Want to see what Mommy can do?" she asked, juggling the balls.

Fallon followed with bright-eyed fascination.

"The trick is running through calculations at the same time. If an HH-60H Seahawk leaves S.C.I. at

1000 hours, flying at a maximum air speed of one hundred and eighty knots, how long— Oops!" The orange bounced across the desk, rolling into the flower vase. Hannah averted disaster. Almost. She caught the vase, but she'd dropped several balls today. "The idea is to keep all the balls in the air. And the answer is he never should have made it."

Setting her juggling act aside, she plucked the card from the flowers. *You've taken command of my heart. Love Peter.*

"Shoot!" It looked like she had a man caught in those crosshairs after all.

CHAPTER FOUR

OFFICERS' CLUB NORTH ISLAND
Coronado, California

"WAITING FOR Lieutenant Commander Stanton?" Mike strode up to the lieutenant, impatiently cooling his heels at the curb outside the Officers' Club.

"Sir. Yes, sir." Spencer "Hollywood" Holden acknowledged Mike with a sharp salute, but he was trying too hard in Mike's opinion. He still had a hard time believing the former child-star hadn't joined the Navy as some sort of publicity stunt.

"Not anymore," Mike said, returning the salute. "Dismissed, Lieutenant."

"Sir?"

"Lend me the getup. Sword and gloves."

Holden complied without question. Good thing, because Mike wasn't in the mood for insubordination.

Stripped of his gear, Hannah's co-pilot didn't seem so Tom Cruise cocky. Which made up for Mike having to stretch the white gloves and let the belt out a notch. But both would do in a pinch.

Even without the added flash of his Full Dress

medals, anyone could see by his ribbon résumé he was a highly decorated officer. A highly decorated officer making an ass of himself over a woman. Hell, he was in good company. For centuries men had waged entire wars over women. And Mike was in the mood for a fight.

Holden disappeared inside, and Mike took the lieutenant's place curbside. Somewhere between Hannah's abrupt departure and the drive over, he'd decided that if she had something to say to him, he wanted to hear it. Even if it was "Take your go-to-hell watch and shove it."

He owed her that much at least.

Identifying the HCS-9 staff car by the Night Hawks flag as it pulled to the curb, he opened the door and offered his arm. "Spence—" she began, using him as leverage, only to be brought nose to shoulder board with his gold epaulet. She snatched her hand back as if from a snake. Once bitten, twice shy?

He tried not to take it personally; SEALs were called snake eaters, but never cold-blooded reptiles. Besides just her touch was enough to warm his blood.

"Sorry, not Holden," he drawled. "Disappointed? And here I strapped on my sword just for you." Or rather commandeered it.

"If I'd known, I would have worn my strap on."

"Now *that* I'd like to see."

"Then it's too bad a lady has no need for a tempered-steel phallic symbol."

That sounded more like the Hannah he knew and…missed. He let loose a hearty chuckle. How long had it been since he'd felt like laughing? How long had it been since they'd last exchanged banter? "From what I hear the lady created quite a stir arriving at the Change of Command Ceremony unescorted."

"So they drafted you to be my handler?"

"This is an all-volunteer Navy."

She raised a perfect eyebrow. "Speaking of volunteers, what have you done with Spence?"

"Ordered him to get lost."

"Rank has its privileges?"

"Absolutely."

That, and the green-eyed monster had reared its ugly head. Holden had been her co-pilot for at least the four years Mike had known her. He wasn't so cynical that he believed men and women couldn't be friends, but in his experience sex always got in the way.

More staff cars pulled up to the curb and he crooked his elbow. "Shall we?"

RHIP. His rank left her little choice but to accept his offered arm. She acquiesced, latching on to his biceps, and he measured his stride to hers. Although her legs were long and lovely, they weren't as long as his.

The side boys opened the double doors.

"Ladies first," he insisted, pressing a hand to the small of her back to keep that contact as he guided her toward the cloakroom.

Once inside, they removed their headgear and

gloves, or in his case Holden's, securing them inside their covers. Hannah handed them off to the hatcheck girl while Mike removed the scabbard and exchanged the ensemble for the ticket.

"Separate tickets, please," Hannah insisted, fluffing out her hair.

"If you insist."

"I insist."

The hatcheck girl was riveted by their conversation. Mike took the second ticket but didn't offer it to Hannah right away.

"I have three hundred guests waiting," she prompted.

"Before your mother and sister came along, you were about to say something…."

"Mike, not here." She glanced at the girl behind him and cleared her throat. "Given the fact we'll be working together, I think we should keep it strictly professional."

He didn't care about the girl, but Hannah was lucky. The next wave of guests entered the building, leaving him little choice but to respect her wishes. "If that's what you want."

"That's what I want."

That's not what her eyes were saying as they held his gaze and wouldn't let go. Or maybe he was the one who couldn't let go. "Why didn't you tell me your father was a Navy SEAL?"

"You've been talking to my mother. What's there to tell? I barely remember him."

"I'm sorry, Han." He didn't even know what he was apologizing for—her father's death, his own disappearing act, or both. How could he explain his fear of hurting her when that's exactly what he'd done?

"Are we through with apologies?"

"I guess we are. And since we're being so PC, *Commander,* I'll expect a formal call at your earliest convenience." He had no intention of letting this conversation go.

"Fine. May I have the ticket, please? I'm a big girl and can make it to the party on my own. I'll call you if I need an escort, Commander."

Ouch! He handed over the ticket, more than ready to abandon his duty. But he couldn't let her go in there unarmed. "Han, word of advice for getting along with these guys. If you're going to rock the boat, think gentle waves."

POSITIONED NEXT TO Captain Loring, behind the giant sheet cake with the Night Hawks logo, Hannah mustered a smile for the camera.

Think gentle waves and rocking boats.

Capsized was more like it. Seeing McCaffrey today had turned hers upside down. *There was something* she wanted to tell him, but couldn't without rocking several boats.

The enlisted Photographer's Mate snapped the photo capturing her frown. "One more of the two of you cutting the cake," he insisted.

Loring dipped his sword into the first slice as they both held on to the handle. "I don't see your mother, Hannah?"

Hannah cast a sidelong glance at the man just as the photographer took his next snapshot. "Hold for one more," he said again.

If she didn't manage a smile, they'd be here all day.

"She's driving over with my sister and the baby in our car. It's easier than switching Fallon's car seat back and forth."

"Will your mother be in the San Diego area long?"

"Until the end of next week."

"Maybe she'll have time for dinner with an old friend." He smiled into the camera.

Her mom and Captain Loring? Friends? Now that would take some getting used to. A slower, less certain smile spread across Hannah's face. "Maybe."

"Got it!" the photographer said.

Before the polite applause ended, she found herself searching the O Club for her mother and sister. "Sammy! Over here!" Hannah waved her through the door of the crowded banquet room. "Where's Fallon?"

"Fallon's cranky. Mom had me drive them home."

"Oh." Hannah quickly hid her disappointment. With McCaffrey here maybe it was for the best. "I should go, too."

At home she could look into her daughter's

eyes, where the reason for keeping father and daughter apart made sense. She didn't want to hurt either of them. But it was a decision already causing her pain.

"No way, this is your big day. Besides, you promised to introduce me to Spencer Holden. I've only been in love with him forever."

Like every other groupie.

Holden had caused quite a stir when he'd walked away from the fame and fortune of Hollywood to enroll in an Ivy League college. A few years later he'd walked into a Navy recruiting office. The paparazzi still followed him around as if he were Elvis.

At first Hannah had found it all amusing, but it soon became annoying. And now her own sister had joined the ranks of the starstruck.

Sammy leaned back against the bar and surveyed the room. "Wow! Are all these guys single?"

"Not *all*." Hannah was too jaded not to see past a well-cut uniform—with one exception of course, and he seemed to have disappeared. Finally she could relax. Except Sammy had that kid-in-a-candy-store look that made Hannah want to rush her sister from the O Club *before* she bit into the goodies.

"Excuse me, Lieutenant Commander Stanton." Lieutenant Russell Parish, her Executive Officer squeezed through the crowd and came toward them.

"Yes, Russ, what is it?" He stopped next to Sammy, who had eyes only for Spence and every other pilot out on the dance floor.

"Ma'am." Russ acknowledged Sammy as he reached across her to hand Hannah his calling card.

Sammy shifted her gaze to give Russ the once-over, but dismissed the crew-cut pilot for other more appealing eye candy.

Russ was too well mannered to take offense. "When would you like me to come calling, ma'am?" This time the "ma'am" was directed at Hannah.

"Why don't I have my social secretary call you?"

Parish's eyes skittered to her sister, but he didn't so much as smile. "Yes, ma'am." He spared another "ma'am" and a nod to Sammy before he moved away.

"What a geek," Sammy said when he was out of earshot.

Privately Hannah agreed, but he was a geek who followed protocol. She handed Sammy the card. "There are going to be more of these."

"Give me a break. I'm not drop-dead gorgeous. I'm not tall. Or thin. Or you."

"What's that supposed to mean?"

"Nothing. Forget it."

Sammy had put on the freshman fifteen in college. Then another as she'd settled into teaching at the elementary level. And another during a rotten relationship that had been a blessing in disguise for Hannah and Fallon—Sammy's need to "get away" had coincided with Hannah's need for a nanny— But Hannah had never realized until now that the highs and lows in her sister's life were marked by weight gain. Or that her sister might be unhappy about that.

Hannah gave her sister a squeeze. "I think you're beautiful."

"Just what every gal wants to hear," Sammy said, but she squeezed back.

"Regardless, there will be more of these. Squadron Officers have to call on the new CO." She softened the blow to Sammy's ego with a smile.

"Back up, you're saying they have to call on you?"

"It gives me a chance to talk with them one-on-one." Just like she had a duty to call on her superiors. As McCaffrey had been so quick to point out, she'd only managed to put off the inevitable confrontation. From here on out they moved in the same social and professional stratosphere. Avoiding him was out of the question.

At least she had the lunch with Lu to look forward to. Officers' wives tended to exclude female officers from their circles, but then so did their husbands. Rarely did she experience the day-to-day camaraderie her male counterparts relished.

With the exception of her co-pilot, fellow pilots were respectful but guarded around her. Like her XO. Which was fine. She wasn't interested in anything but a professional relationship with them. She should have extended her rule to include the SEALs they shuttled. Of course she'd never felt the need for such a rule before.

"So we're going to have a parade of single guys over for dinner?"

"It doesn't have to be dinner."

"Are you kidding? I love to cook," Sammy said with a cat-that-swallowed-the-canary grin.

"Sammy, do not consider my command your personal dating service."

Her sister fanned herself with Parish's card. "I think I'm going to like being your nanny, Hannah."

"DRINKING ALONE? And before noon?" Admiral Bell pulled up a stool next to Mike.

"You know I take my drinking seriously." Mike automatically checked his bare wrist, then dug out the watch from his pocket. "Besides, it's after noon."

By six seconds.

And sitting at this bar kept him out of the main banquet hall. Out of sight, out of mind. Yeah, right.

At least the lights and the music were lower in here, which suited his mood.

"Nice watch," Warren commented as Mike strapped his shackle back on. "Since when do commanders make more than admirals?"

"It was a gift."

"Nice gift. Chase-Durer, the military pilot's watch of choice." Warren picked up on details like that. Mike could only imagine the conclusions the man had already drawn. "How long after you received *the gift* before you started running?"

Mike snorted back a half laugh. Warren knew him too well. "I started running before," he admitted.

"You must have really liked this one." Leaving

Mike to sort out his conflicting thoughts on the subject, the admiral ordered a rye. "A double. And another round for the Commander here," he said to the bartender, even though Mike was still nursing his first beer.

He did like Hannah. That was the problem.

After their drinks were lined up, the admiral dispensed with the small talk. "I saved you a seat. What happened?"

"Got back late from San Clemente."

"So I heard. Something about a case of ouzo exchanging hands." Warren nodded in the direction of a young airman.

"What the hell?" Mike watched said case go by on the shoulder of the enlisted man. "Tell Norton I'm going to kick his ass if he pulls a stunt like that again," Mike called after the kid. The airman stepped up his pace and Mike had no doubt the message would be delivered to HCS-5 along with the B. Stefanouris. "So that's how she did it."

"Which is beside the point. What the hell were you doing on S.C.I. to begin with? I told you to have your team stand down."

"We were standing down."

Despite Warren's bluster, the admiral had been kept apprised of Mike's whereabouts. And Mike had kept up with the more mundane tasks of being a Commanding Officer.

"I know the demons driving you, Mac. Maybe you don't want a break, but your men deserve one."

"I gave them the option. They volunteered for SCI."

Warren set down his drink. "With everything hanging over their heads right now, I guess I can't blame them."

Mike scrubbed a weary hand over his face. "We lost two good men last time out. Then came home and—" he shook his head because he still couldn't quite believe it "—now Nash is accused of killing his pregnant wife in some posttraumatic-stress-disorder episode."

"There was an eyewitness. The sister-in-law—"

"Nash didn't kill his wife." Mike defended his men as hotly as they fought for him in battle. "But he's being called a monster and looking at life from behind bars while his newborn son fights for his."

"Kenneth Nash had his day in court, Mac."

And thankfully still had a few appeals to run through. "Nash is—" Mike shrugged off the present tense he'd been about to use and replaced it with the past "—*was* one of the few married men on my team. The others are scared of the fear they see in their wives' eyes. And the rest of us don't even have that much to go home to." *Thank God.* Mike swiveled to look at Warren. "Trust me to know what's best for my team." And right now that was keeping them busy.

The eyewitness was wrong. Nash would have come to him if he'd thought he was losing it. Because of their ingrained buddy system, SEALs had a low rate of PTSD. They served as a team. They went into ops together and they came out together. Homecomings were quiet affairs, and while home they were each other's support system.

The other services were just now learning this.

But what if Mike was wrong? What if Nash had lost it?

Wasn't he himself on edge? Feeling unsettled?

"All right, Mac. You win. But since you can't show up on time and without ants in your pants I've decided that instead of Team One, I'm sending your team to Nevada to work with the new Commander of HCS-9."

"Are you shittin' me?"

"You have a problem with that?"

"Other than I'd rather donate another pint of blood to the Middle East, none at all." Telling the admiral his problem with the Commander wasn't an option. So he sucked it up and polished off his beer.

Warren stirred his drink, clinking the ice against the glass. "You know her old man was a SEAL."

Mike nodded. Rosemary Stanton had said as much. She'd also told him her husband had died on a training op. After 'Nam. But that was all the information she'd volunteered. Maybe that was all she knew.

Training op was often code for undisclosed mission. Like the Shadow War in Laos that started before and ended after Vietnam.

It sure as hell wasn't a two-week boondoggle in Nevada.

"What was he like?"

"Van Stanton?" The admiral looked thoughtful as

he tapped into his memories. "Wide receiver for the U of Wisconsin-Oshkosh Titans. Nationally ranked player. Good, but not good enough. Instead of being drafted into the NFL he was drafted into the Navy. Though I don't remember him as being the type to look back on what might have been."

"That wasn't my question."

"He was a lot like you, Mac. One hundred and ten percent in the game. Whether that game was football or shadow ops."

Mike cursed under his breath. It wasn't what he'd wanted to hear, but it was what he needed to know. He glanced across the bar and had to do a double take. Hannah was doling out cash to the bartender, probably for the case of B. Stefanouris.

Calypso's signature drink. She wanted rid of him that bad, huh? She caught sight of him and returned his bold stare. He raised his beer in salute. She nodded, but without that teasing light in her eyes he'd grown accustomed to seeing over the years. Was he responsible for putting that light out?

Why had she wanted him in the first place?

And why was he driving himself crazy wanting her? He'd been the one to walk, or rather run. Coward.

Warren's gaze followed. "Trust me to know what's best for my Teams." He threw Mike's words back at him, emphasizing the plural. "You're going to Nevada. Whatever's between the two of you, get it worked out. You have two weeks."

Mike knew better than to argue with subtle suggestions that passed for bona fide orders. Warren whipped out his wallet and enough bills to cover the tab. "Do the right thing, Mac."

"PINCH ME so I know I'm not dreaming," Sammy said.

They'd arrived home that evening with a stack of calling cards. Hannah turned the key in the lock and pushed the door open. "You're dreaming."

"I don't know. Mr. and Mrs. Spencer Holden has a nice ring to it, don't you think? Or is that Lieutenant and Mrs. Spencer Holden?"

"Don't start sending out the invitations just yet." Sammy had managed to corner Spence. The pair had danced a couple of times. But she failed to acknowledge that he'd danced with every other female in the room. Except Hannah, who'd politely refused.

"A girl can window-shop, can't she?"

Hannah flipped on the light switch in the entry hall. "That depends. For the dress or the man? With the right shoes a little black number can do wonders. But you don't need a man to make you whole. You know that, don't you?"

"I may not need him, but I want him," Sammy said, missing the point entirely. "Besides if he doesn't want me, there's always one of these guys." She rattled off a couple names. Then stopped at one card. "That Marine, Hunter, wasn't half-bad—he really stood out in a room full of sailors. And of course, Parish," she said with a snort, having reached the bottom of the pile. "Did you notice his receding hair-line? I give the guy ten years tops before he's a total cue ball."

"Some men look good bald."

"He's not one of them."

"Don't go screwing with my XO's head—" Hannah hung her purse on a peg near the door, but stopped in the middle of removing her jacket. The house remained unusually quiet except for the soft sound of someone crying.

"Mom?" Hannah called out as she ran through the bare living room and up the stairs toward her own bedroom and the baby's Portacrib. When she entered, Fallon was sound asleep. Her mother sat in a dark corner, rocking the single chair in the room and hugging the flag.

Hannah knew those private tears too well. She wanted to tell her mother it was okay to cry. But she knew her mother wouldn't think so.

"Mom, it's okay to talk about him." *I want to talk about him.* "I know you must miss him." *I miss him, too.*

But I'm afraid I can't remember him.

Please, help me remember him.

"I'm fine," her mother said, blotting her eyes with a perfectly folded tissue. Because her mother did everything perfectly. One fold for every blow. Which was exactly three times. Then dry eyes and a stiff upper lip. "It's just being back here after all these years. Everything is the same, and so different."

Hannah sat down on the window seat, ignoring the ocean view she'd paid such a pretty penny for. "Captain Loring asked why you weren't at the reception. I didn't realize you two knew each other."

"You were probably too young to remember. But JJ and Liz were our neighbors when we lived in Navy Housing all those years ago. Of course, Liz is gone now, as well."

"I don't remember," Hannah confessed. Those happy days were lost to her, locked up somewhere too painful to remember.

CHAPTER FIVE

PETER PETRONE ARRIVED by taxicab the following morning. Hannah stepped out her front door just in time to watch the cab pull away from the curb. "Peter?"

"You sound surprised."

"I am."

He wandered up her walkway, briefcase in hand, summer-weight suit jacket flung over his arm. His wrinkled pants, rolled-up sleeves and loose tie had been the norm since college. "Don't I get a hug?"

"Of course." She stepped into his outstretched arms.

She'd never slept with him, but her college roommate had. Sydney claimed she couldn't resist that boyish dimpled grin. Personally Hannah liked the rumpled blond hair and intelligent green eyes behind the wire-framed rims.

The three of them had taken aerospace engineering courses together at CU Boulder—go Buffs—but only one of them was a genius. Syd had dropped out of aerospace altogether. Hannah, a typical overachiever, had worked hard for every grade she got. For her it had been all about flying anyway.

But for Peter the laws of physics and how to defy them came naturally. He'd had offers from Boeing, Lockheed-Martin and NASA before he'd even graduated. Instead he'd joined forces with a small Boulder-based company, making Hall-Petrone Aerospace Tech and himself rich with his patents.

She pulled back and looked into his eyes, still wondering what the hell he was doing here.

"Look at you," he said. "So this is what all the well-dressed pilots are wearing to wage war?"

"Drab olive-green is always in season," she said through tight lips. She knew what was coming next.

"I wish you'd change your mind, Hannah. Come home."

"It's not a matter of changing my mind. My mind is made up. It's my duty to be here."

"And is it your duty to get yourself killed halfway around the world? For what?"

"I'm not going to debate foreign policy or politics with you, Peter. I made my commitment to the reserves long before I came to work for you. Please, let's just agree to disagree on the subject. You didn't fly all this way for an argument, did you? Why are you here?"

"I told you I was flying in for the weekend."

She tried hard to remember their hurried phone conversation. "You may have said something," she conceded. Clearly she'd misunderstood. "But, Peter, I have a job to do. The work doesn't get put on hold just because it's Saturday." Not when she had to ready the squadron to deploy on Monday. And she was already late for her first day as Commanding Officer. What an impression that would make. "I don't have time to entertain company. I have to get to the base—"

"I could tag along," he offered hopefully.

Hannah almost groaned out loud. A male tagging along was not the image she wanted to present to her squadron her first day at the helm. "That's really not a good idea."

"Not for the whole day, just to the base. I scheduled a meeting at the Naval Amphibious Base with a Rear Admiral Bell. He wants a look at the prototype for the fuel cell." Peter tipped his briefcase. "This could be my biggest military contract yet. We can celebrate at dinner."

"And that doesn't seem the least bit hypocritical to you? You object to my contract with the service because it involves personal sacrifice, but you're willing to contract with the service for personal gain."

"Hypocritical? Not at all, not if you're assigned as my Navy liaison. You won't have to fight. And you'll be doing your duty from behind a desk in Colorado. You do want to stay home with Fallon, don't you?"

Oh, great. Now he was going to throw *that* guilt trip at her. He was worse than her mother. Or in league with her. Hannah felt positive she wouldn't feel like being wined and dined this evening. But they needed to talk. Big time. "Peter—"

"I'll take you somewhere nice," he said. "I'm staying at the Hotel Del Coronado. How does the Prince of Wales Room sound for dinner?"

She knew the hotel's restaurant by reputation only. "Like you're going to need a lot of pull." Not to mention a reservation—unless of course you were a gazillionaire with a company named after you about to go public on the NASDAQ, or was it NYSE? She knew he'd get the reservation, but she was more concerned he might actually have enough clout to get her reassigned.

For whatever reason, her personal merit or some admiral wanting to add "politically correct" to his résumé, she'd been given the opportunity to command. She didn't think she'd lose it per one civilian's request. But if she screwed up, the Navy might think she'd be better off serving in another less visible capacity. It would be best if Peter understood her position right from the start.

"Peter," she began again, but before she could argue the point further, McCaffrey pulled up in his battered Jeep.

What was he doing here?

"Need a ride?"

He'd asked that question once before and it had led straight to the bedroom. The end of their two-week drill in Fallon had started out simple enough. She'd stepped out of the Stillwater Inn after checking out, wearing her Summer Whites for travel and carrying her gear. A short while later they were on US-50 headed west. Nothing but sixty miles of open desert road ahead of them.

When she'd almost lost her cover to the wind, he'd given her one of his ST-11 ball caps to wear instead. Today he wore a similar ball cap with his khakis. A knot formed in her stomach as she realized she still had that other one somewhere. She should find it and set it aside for Fallon. Someday her daughter would have questions about her father, and Hannah intended to answer them honestly. Mac was a good man. But like the wind, he couldn't be tied down.

He hopped out of the Jeep. And once again removed his cover in anticipation of her salute.

She pulled her own HCS-9 ball cap down low. She hadn't meant to get caught wearing her flight suit off base. Not that she couldn't wear it to and from work, just that it felt inappropriate to appear that lazy in front of a peer. It was up to her to set the standard for her squadron. She should have worn her khakis into work and changed there.

"Is that your duty driver?" Peter asked as McCaffrey strolled toward them.

A commander, a duty driver? Now that was laughable.

"It's...*him*," was all she said, pleading with her

eyes for Peter to keep his mouth shut. For the moment it worked. "A little out of your way isn't it, Commander? Imperial Beach is on the other side of the base."

"Well, you know, wanted to check out Coronado. See how the other half lives." He eyeballed her new seaside bungalow, sold sign still stuck in the lawn. Then he turned his attention to Peter. "Commander Mike McCaffrey." He extended his hand.

"Peter Petrone."

The two men sized each other up.

"So how much does one of these run?" McCaffrey asked, appraising the lot. "You're Hannah's Realtor, right?"

"No, Hannah and I are—"

"Colleagues," Hannah finished for him, knowing full well Mac was fishing. "Peter flew in from Colorado to discuss a presentation we were working on before I left—"

"*That* Peter Petrone," as if he hadn't known all along. "President and CEO of Hall-Petrone? Should have guessed by the pocket protector."

Peter looked down at his breast pocket. He wasn't wearing a pocket protector.

Hannah scowled at McCaffrey. Fortunately the childish prank went right over Peter's head.

"That's right," Peter said.

"When am I going to get a look at that prototype

for the new fuel cell you're working on?" McCaffrey asked. "I could use something to lighten my load in the field."

Hannah knew from experience that it took about twelve pounds of batteries just to operate a two-way radio for three days, and that didn't even include the rest of his equipment.

"What do you pack for a typical three-day mission?" Peter asked. "About one hundred pounds of batteries and equipment?"

"You've done your homework."

"I can't do anything about the rest, but the fuel cell is going to cut your total weight by half. Our two-pound version is about the size of a video cassette and has enough power to run all your field equipment for three days. I have a meeting with a Rear Admiral Bell at the Naval Amphibious Base this morning."

"What time?"

"Late morning. Ten-ish."

"What do you say I show you around the base courtesy of Uncle Sam, tag along to that meeting, and then we hook up with Lieutenant Commander Stanton for lunch at the O Club?"

"Sounds good." Peter accepted the invitation.

McCaffrey led Peter toward the Jeep. While macho man hopped in the driver's side, Peter looked for the passenger door. When he realized there wasn't one, he climbed in. "Hannah, aren't you coming?" he asked.

But it was McCaffrey whose gaze challenged her.

And to that she answered, "I'll take my own car, thanks."

NAVAL AIR STATION NORTH ISLAND
Coronado, California

BY THE TIME Hannah arrived at Hangar Nine, she'd missed morning muster and her chance to address the squadron as planned. *No apologies. No excuses.* Men in charge didn't make them and neither would she. She repeated the mantra several more times while walking from her car to the building.

As she passed by her yeoman's desk, the young man stationed in the outer office popped to attention, catching her by surprise. Since leaving her active duty days behind, she'd forgotten more military protocol than she'd ever remember.

"Morning," Hannah said in passing.

"Good morning, ma'am. The XO is in your office."

"As you were." The order came more easily than she thought it would. She'd called Parish from her cell phone to give him a heads-up. Since she'd already been running late, she'd taken a few extra minutes to drive by Navy Housing—though all her Executive Officer needed to know was that she'd be late. Once she'd reached the San Diego neighborhood where she'd lived as a child, she'd realized it might be impossible to find the house without a street address.

They'd all looked alike.

Most flew the flag. Some bore a yellow ribbon, waiting for their serviceman or -woman to return.

But instinct had her parking at a corner lot.

There'd been signs of young children everywhere.

From the primary-colored toys scattered throughout the yard, to the drawings hanging in the picture window, it looked and felt like a real home.

Hannah had just sat there taking it all in. The front door opened. Not wanting to be caught spying, she'd put the car in gear and rolled forward. But as she'd stolen one last glance in the rearview mirror, tears stung her eyes as a Naval officer had kissed his wife and daughters goodbye.

She pushed aside the recollection.

Parish stood as she entered her office. She caught his almost imperceptible glance toward the wall clock.

No apologies. No excuses.

"Good morning, Lieutenant." She hung up her purse on the coatrack in the corner.

"Ma'am." Her XO handed over the daily SOPAs. "We're monitoring a promising situation in the Gulf," he said.

Hannah looked up from scanning the dailies. "How promising?" she asked, already headed for the ready room. Seahawks were the military equivalent of ambulance chasers. Because the Army had so many more Blackhawks, and even the Air Force had both Pave Hawks and the newer and better equipped Pave Lows to do the job, sometimes it was a matter of Seahawks being in the right place at the right time.

"Attention on deck." Her crew chief, Webb Emerson, called the room to attention.

Spence stopped mid-strum on his guitar. Boomer, her door gunner, nudged the co-pilot to his feet. Also standing at attention were Parish's crew. Chief Kai Makani, gunner Christian Quinn and co-pilot, Second Lieutenant Ethan "Hawkeye" Hunter on loan from the Marine Corps. With the exception of Hunter, she'd worked with these guys for years. Her crew of reservists drilled out of Buckley Airfield in Colorado and were from the four corners of the west.

"As you were, gentleman."

The ready room contained everything for those long waits between flights. Ping-Pong table, beverage-stocked refrigerator, a bookcase full of paperback novels and an assortment of gunmetal-gray tables and chairs. Someone had donated an old couch to stretch out on. The once beige upholstery had been worn to a less discriminating color and two paperbacks replaced the right front leg.

The cots in the back room were a better bet for rest. At least the light and noise levels were lower. Of course that was relative in a naval air station with jets and helos flying overhead.

In one corner a police scanner monitored local emergency communications, while another scanner monitored the Coast Guard. A handy two-way radio ensured they could respond to either. There were six TVs of various makes and models mounted around the room, one tuned into local news, four to cable news networks, and one played ESPN 24/7.

Today they ignored the Padre's game in favor of CNN. They were eager for her to give them the word to go.

Taking off her ball cap, she held it with the clip-board in her hands as she watched the story unfold on-screen. The situation in the Persian Gulf warranted closer observation. "Give Norton a heads-up," she said to Parish, even though she could guarantee HCS-5 would already be on it. "This one goes to Five, guys. We have to be in Nevada on Monday. But find out what SPECWAR has to say on the situation," she called over her shoulder to her XO. Spence followed her back to her office. She could tell it was him by the jangle of spurs he wore with his boots.

"Those aren't regulation." She stopped and held her office door for him. He preceded her inside. Guitar strapped to his back, Stetson in hand, Spencer Holden took the steel-cowboy image to the extreme.

"Since when did you turn into such a hard ass?"

"It comes with the desk. Seriously, Spence, it's not all fun and games anymore. We're here in the first place because it's real. I want to see regulation boots on those feet when you're in uniform."

"I'll trade you my spurs for your breast pump."

"Excuse me?"

He rattled the prescription bottle of quinine on her desk. "You haven't taken a single one. You've been pumping more than iron from the looks of things?"

Hannah pushed the flower vase aside and plopped down on her desktop, clipboard and cap resting on her knee. "You need to mind your own business."

"My pilot is my business."

He opened and closed desk drawers. When he reached for the bottom right, she leaned over and slammed it shut. "All right," she agreed. "Breast pump out, malaria pills in. But you're going to *give* me those spurs for safekeeping."

"But I keep the hat." He put it on, adjusting the angle and his grin until he had them both just right. It was easy to see why half the female population was in love with him. The other half was just plain crazy.

"Deal." She extended her hand and they shook on it. "You can even keep the little lady." She modified their bargain to include his favorite six-string. "I wouldn't expect you to leave home without her." Her smile faded at the thought of all she'd be leaving behind. "She's so little. I'm afraid she's going to forget me."

"Not a chance." Spence was the keeper of her secrets and her insecurities. But being able to read her mind was what made him such a good co-pilot. Of course he was the only one in her squadron who knew McCaffrey was Fallon's father.

"Just blame it on postpartum hormones and my mother," she apologized. "See, I'm going to start taking the pills." She opened the bottle and tapped one into her palm. "First she insists on coming to California, which was fine, I wanted her here for the

Change of Command Ceremony. But now that she's here, she spends all of her time moping around the house."

He opened the minifridge and handed her a bottled water. Spence had never met her mother or sister, at least not until yesterday, but he made a good sounding board.

"Thank you." She washed down the quinine with a grimace. It had been almost thirty years since her mother had packed up every last reminder of her father and started a new life for them in Colorado.

But here…his ghost was everywhere.

There were no cardboard boxes to hold those memories. If she didn't think it would cause her mother more pain, Hannah would have insisted on opening some of those boxes a long time ago.

Or was it a little girl's pain she wanted to keep stowed away? What was it she'd read recently about memory and expressive language? Humans had the capacity to remember back to the womb, but no language to express it. Which was why memories from the formative ages of three or four were often the first recalled…

Hannah closed her eyes, searching for that three- or four-year-old. *"Push me higher, Daddy. Higher!" Strong hands grabbed hold, then let go.*

Did that mean she couldn't express her feelings for her father beyond that of a seven-year-old? Sometimes it seemed that way. She crumpled the water bottle.

Spence propped himself beside her on the desk

and fiddled with his guitar strings. "I take it you haven't told him yet?"

"*Him* being McCaffrey? No," she confessed. When it came to McCaffrey, the language didn't exist to express what she felt.

Spence strummed a few loose bars of "Crusin'." Her signature song when she flew was "Playing With The Boys." But sometimes after she dropped McCaffrey and his boys off, she hit the play button for something a little less *Top Gun* and more Smokey Robinson—even if it was the Gwyneth Paltrow, Huey Lewis version from the movie *Duets.*

Her co-pilot might tease her about Mac and movie soundtracks, but next time out she'd pay him back with a pop tune from his teen idol days, complete with crew sing-along.

"Got anything cold to drink?" a booming voice called out. "Hey, Calypso. Hey, Hollywood. Fridge in the ready room is on the fritz again." Boomer strode in on the last few notes, stuck his head in the minifridge and helped himself to a soda. "Is Hollywood giving you a hard time, Commander? Ask him about *his* Navy nurse—the one who thought he was Dougie Howser—"

Spence shoved Boomer toward the exit. "Take a hike."

"The door was open," Boomer protested. "Thanks." He toasted Hannah with the can of Mountain Dew on the way out.

"A girlfriend? A Navy nurse girlfriend? We've only been here—what, five days?"

Spence closed the door behind Boomer and sagged against it, laughing. "I'm glad you got a kick out of that. Come on, do I look anything thing like that Howser kid?"

"That's what makes it so funny." She smiled. "How come you've never mentioned her before?"

"Because we just sleep together. And I never tell you about any of the women I just sleep with." He waggled his brows. "Don't want to appear as shallow as I really am."

"You're the least shallow good-looking man I know."

"Just not as complex as *him?*"

Hannah sobered, suspicious of where Spence was going with this. "He has a name, you know."

"I know he's good at leaving, and you're good at leaving things left unsaid."

She definitely didn't like where he was going with this.

He pushed to his feet, tossed her the bottle of quinine, and headed for the door. "Talk to Mac. Talk to your mom. Now is not the time to leave things unsaid…we're here because it's real."

Spence left her with that bitter pill to swallow. Sometimes she really hated that he wasn't afraid to call her on the bullshit. McCaffrey was a complicated man. Their whole situation was complicated. Was she making it better or worse by not telling him about their daughter?

No apologies. No excuses.

The rest of the morning passed slowly, most of it spent at her desk. Hannah checked her watch, impatient for a return call from the CO of SEAL Team One. His yeoman had said he'd be out of the office until later that afternoon. There were some last-minute details she wanted to iron out before reaching Nevada. But she suspected, like McCaffrey, all the SEAL Team COs were in that meeting with Peter and the admiral.

She'd debated putting in a call to Admiral Bell to head off Peter's request that she be the liaison between Hall-Petrone and the Navy. But she didn't want to run to the admiral with every minor problem. Surely he could see the position was a major conflict of interest for her. Then again maybe it wasn't. Somebody had to do the job. Maybe she was a fool for not jumping on the opportunity.

Colorado, a playpen in her office…and no McCaffrey.

Or California, a command post, no playpen, but…what? McCaffrey?

CHAPTER SIX

OFFICERS' CLUB NORTH ISLAND
Coronado, California

WHEN HANNAH SHOWED UP at the O Club dressed in her khakis, McCaffrey was seated at a table for two by himself. She should have suspected something like this from Mac.

Taking a deep breath, she approached the table. "What have you done with him?"

"Petrone?" He feigned innocence. "Don't look at me as if I stuffed the body somewhere. North Island *is* the birthplace of Naval aviation and the largest aerospace facility in the world. He got sidetracked. You know the type."

"I'm leaving."

"I outmaneuvered you, that's all." McCaffrey nudged the chair with his toe. "Sit. We need to talk."

She was about to refuse when the waiter came up behind her and pulled the chair out all the way. "Thank you," she said as he placed a menu in front of her. To Mac she said, "I'm only staying because I'm hungry."

"Of course," he agreed from behind the menu. "But as long as you're staying…we need to talk."

Hannah's heart hammered her chest. No telling what information McCaffrey had managed to pump from Peter. And Peter being, well, Peter, and Mac being a snake, poor Peter probably didn't even know he'd been squeezed.

If McCaffrey knew about the baby, he was certainly playing it cool.

She could play cool herself. "About?"

He didn't answer, forcing her to look up from her menu to gauge his mood. If anything, he looked as starved as she felt. "About Petrone."

Relief flooded through her. "Oh, him."

"Oh, him?" he echoed in disbelief. "Are you two lovers, or what?"

"That's none of your business." *Or what?* He had her on the defensive, but she didn't owe him an explanation.

"I'll take that as a no. Give the guy a clue, because he doesn't have one."

Hannah sat back in her chair. Mac never sat in a chair, he draped himself all over it. The relaxed confidence belied the restless energy. It was one of the things she liked best about him. But upon closer inspection, he seemed a touch edgy today. "If I didn't know better, McCaffrey, I'd say you were jealous."

"Who says I'm not?"

Not in a million years would he admit something like that if he really meant it. "Jealousy would imply that you actually engaged your emotions."

"Bitterness would imply that I'd actually engaged

yours," he countered. "Is that all we have left, Han, jealousy and bitterness?"

No, there is something else.

The mythical Calypso died grieving Odysseus when he left after seven years. Hannah knew better than to engage her emotions for more than seven minutes with a Navy SEAL. She worked with these guys, she knew what they were like and what the job entailed. If a gal got one to stick around for more than seven days at a stretch, it was only because she was putting out *and* doing his laundry.

Some might even call that a marriage. Not her.

She could make McCaffrey her captive with four little words—*we have a daughter.* What she couldn't do was keep him. In seven months, or seven days, or the next time she turned around, he'd be gone. Again.

"What were we thinking?" she wondered out loud. "You're the best mistake of my life, Mike. Just not one I'd care to repeat."

"We can get past mistakes."

"To where? I'm a thirty-three-year-old woman, soon to be thirty-four, looking for not one or even two nights, but a commitment from a man. Doesn't that scare the hell out of you, McCaffrey?"

"It should scare the hell out of you."

"You're right, it should and it does. Because while you were gone, I got a look at our future, and you weren't even a part of it. I can't see either of us changing to fit the other, can you?"

"I thought we were a pretty good fit already."

"That's because you don't even know how much I've changed already. A year's a long time to wait for somebody who couldn't be bothered to pick up a phone."

"It wasn't like—"

"What was it like? Don't tell me you've been deep cover, incommunicado for the past twelve months. I might even want to believe you, but you can't play that card with me…I'd know it's a lie."

"I never meant to hurt you, Han."

"You did. I'm over it. I'm not bitter, Mike. I'm disappointed. I thought we had something, something that doesn't have anything to do with jealousy. But I was wrong, we're the proverbial two ships passing in the night."

The waiter arrived to take their orders. "Ah…chicken Caesar salad, dressing on the side, and an iced tea, lemon on the side. Thank you," she said, snapping the menu shut.

"Burger, *rare*." McCaffrey placed his order. He sat back. His gaze fixed on her until she felt like raw meat.

"This is dutch," she clarified.

"Isn't it always?"

"I was just making sure you knew—"

"That some things haven't changed. Like me for example? And the fact that you're still stubborn when it comes to letting a man pick up the check. Not everything has changed, Han."

That was part of the problem, too. Though she

didn't want to look for that common ground. Unable to hold up under his intense scrutiny, she spread her napkin across her lap before meeting his eyes again. "Why don't I pick up the tab?" Which just about summed up their relationship.

"That supposed to bother me?"

"Not if you're secure in your masculinity."

"You can try on the pants all you want, sweetheart. But it doesn't change a thing when they come off."

"Like that's ever going to happen."

"It happened."

"I meant again," she corrected, angry that he'd called her on it. The waiter returned and set their glasses in front of them. She held her peace until he left them alone. "You know," she said, ripping open two packets of sweetener. "I would enjoy this meal a lot more if we didn't even *attempt* a conversation."

"We're going to have to attempt a whole hell of a lot more than conversation. Bell switched Teams Eleven and One in the training rotation. We're going to be spending the next two weeks together in Fallon, Nevada."

She paused with the packets over her iced tea. "You can't be serious?"

"Apparently not."

Tears pricked the back of her eyes. Maybe bitterness *was* all she had left. "You know, I'm not very hungry after all. You can pick up the tab on this one." She threw her napkin down and left.

MIKE'S APPETITE disappeared with Hannah. The best mistake of her life? How about the biggest mistake of his! He'd stopped to catch his breath when he should have kept right on running.

He tossed his own napkin to the table and was about to push to his feet when he spotted Petrone headed his way.

"Great," he mumbled under his breath, but kept his seat and pasted on a smile. When he'd shown up at Hannah's door this morning, he hadn't expected to find Petrone there. He didn't need a visual of other men in her life.

"There you are." Peter greeted him like a long-lost friend. "Sorry I took so long. Where's Hannah?"

"She had to leave."

"Oh." Peter sounded disappointed.

"How do you feel about chicken Caesar salad?" Mike asked as the waiter approached with two lunches.

Petrone brightened immediately. "I'm sure Hannah had her reasons for leaving."

Mike bit into his burger, knowing full well he was the sole reason. Petrone continued his ode to Hannah. By the time Mike had taken his second bite, Pete had dropped her name six more times. This was going to be a very long lunch.

"I want to thank you for showing me around this morning, I know you're a busy man. That was a nice gesture."

"You're welcome, Pete."

"The truth is I've been wanting to meet you. Now I know why Hannah speaks so highly of you."

Now there was a kick-to-the-gut compliment.

"I hope I've made a favorable impression on you, as well," Petrone continued. "You know, considering... I mean I wouldn't want to get in the middle of anything—"

"No, I don't know. Why don't you jump right in and tell me?"

"My intentions are honorable, I assure you." He dug into his coat pocket and pulled out a velvet box that he snapped open. Mike didn't know much about diamonds, but this one was big and sparkly. The kind most women wanted.

It didn't suit Hannah at all. But maybe she was right, he didn't know her anymore. And that made him the guy without a clue.

"I'm afraid you're not my type, Pete, ol' pal."

"Oh—" Petrone looked confused, then released a nervous laugh "—you're making a joke. You are making a joke, right? Tonight at dinner I'm going to ask Hannah to marry me. I know I don't have to ask, but considering...you know, you two...I was kind of hoping for your blessing."

"*My* blessing?"

"I'm looking forward to being a husband...and a father, you don't have to worry about that." Peter continued his litany of good qualities. "I'll be there for her. I'll provide for her..."

In summary, Pete could give Hannah everything Mike couldn't. Even Hannah's mother must approve of this guy. Not to mention this guy's bank account. Keeping the smile plastered on his face was the hardest thing Mike had ever done. And he'd done some pretty hard things in his life.

Tomorrow wasn't in his vocabulary; neither were words like *future* and *forever.* He lived in the here and now. And Hannah was here, now. As selfish as it sounded, he didn't want to just give up on that. He might be the wrong long-term guy, but he was in the top ten of short-term flings—okay, number one.

"What do you think?" Peter paused long enough to ask.

Mike sat back in his chair. He thought long and hard, but not too long or too hard, because he knew what he wanted had nothing to do with what Hannah needed. The guy obviously cared about Hannah. He wanted to take care of her and that was a plus, because whether Hannah knew it or not, she really needed to be taken care of. She deserved a guy who'd be there for her and could give her babies and a white picket fence.

Ah, hell, now he was thinking too long and too hard.

"I think you should ask her."

"If you don't mind—" Peter leaned forward "—I have a favor to ask of you…"

HANNAH WOKE at 0400 to Fallon's cries. Despite the hour and her lack of sleep, she looked forward to this time alone with her daughter. It would be their last four-a.m. feeding for at least two weeks. Stifling a yawn, she rolled off the air mattress and onto the floor, literally.

"Is Mama's girl hungry?" She reached into the crib and picked up her daughter from the tear-soaked spot. How long had the baby been crying?

"Hannah?" Sammy stirred across the hall.

A while.

"I've got her." Apparently the hours Hannah had put into the move, the old and the new jobs, the transition from civilian to military life and rejecting men were exhausting.

"There, there, baby girl. Mama's here," she whispered, patting Fallon on the back as she moved her to a dry spot. The movers weren't due to arrive for another week. Until then they were making do with the Portacrib and air mattresses and the few pieces they'd brought with them or had bought since their arrival.

By the time she'd changed the baby's diaper and put her in a dry onesie, soft baby words no longer satisfied Fallon. She was hungry and screaming for her bottle. This had been so much easier when she'd been breast-feeding.

She held Fallon close and found herself humming "Cruisin'," which hadn't left her head since Spence had played it for her this morning. Hannah stepped into her slippers and padded down the stairs. Flipping on the kitchen light, she shuffled to the refrigerator.

"I'll put on some tea," her sister said.

"That would be wonderful," their mother agreed.

"I'm sorry." Hannah grabbed a premade bottle and closed the refrigerator door with her hip. "I'm up now. You two can go back to bed—"

"We want to hear all about your big date." Sammy ran water into the teakettle, while Hannah moved to the microwave.

Peter had gotten down on bended knee in the middle of the Prince of Wales Room. She'd been embarrassed by the whole thing, but she'd felt even worse for him.

"Show me the ring," her mother demanded. "I want to see what it looks like on your finger."

"You knew about this and didn't warn me?" Why did men and mothers think a ring was the answer to everything?

"She helped pick it out. All six carats. We didn't think you'd want anything bigger."

"You, too?" Obviously they didn't know her well enough.

Sammy shrugged as she put the kettle on the stovetop.

"I hate to disappoint you, Mother—" Hannah sat down at the table, adjusting the baby in her arms "—but the only carrots I'll be wearing are the ones Fallon spits up on me."

"Why would I be disappointed?" Her mother scoffed at the suggestion. "I merely offered my assistance to a man who's so in love with my daughter he can't see straight, let alone think straight."

"It's not love, Mother, it's need. And the last thing I need right now is a needy man."

"What about Mac? He's not needy," Sammy chimed in.

"Okay, the second-to-last thing I need right now is a needy man. The very last thing I need is a…"

"Man who'll break your heart," her mother added, not unkindly. "I agree. And there are worse things than going into a marriage with your eyes open. You don't love Peter and he needs you. So what? The man should always be a little more in love with the woman. It evens the odds."

"I've read that," Sammy said, getting down the tea bags from the cupboard. "I think it was in a magazine, or maybe on the Internet."

Fallon had stopped crying to greedily suck on her bottle. Hannah held back enough hormone-generated tears to flood the kitchen.

She couldn't wear a ring in the cockpit.

Not that she wanted a ring, dammit.

She'd been about to say, a man who not only didn't want them but couldn't offer her daughter a safe and secure future even if he did. But wasn't that what Peter had offered? So why had her gaze drifted over his shoulder to the BUD/S on the beach as they attempted their rock portage landing. The wannabe SEALs' struggles had held her attention longer than a man proposing marriage.

She knew she was strong enough to go it alone, but was she being fair to her daughter? Peter had taken the red-eye back to Denver, but he'd left the offer on the table.

Should she reconsider for Fallon's sake?

NAVAL AIR STATION NORTH ISLAND
Coronado, California

"MORNING," MIKE SAID over his shoulder. Arms folded, he checked his watch, 0700. Right on time. He'd give her credit for that and the silent approach, or was it the silent treatment? Either way, he'd smelled her perfume from a quarter mile out. Nothing subtle or sweet about a scent as bold and in-your-face as the woman who wore it.

A storm in the desert.

Hot. Heavy. Fragrant with the beauty of a cactus rose.

"Norton's pissed," she said.

And just as thorny.

She stopped shoulder to shoulder with him. Half-a-dozen C-130 transports were on deck, bellies open and waiting. Forklifts moved between stacked pallets outside the hangars and the planes. Team One had been only too happy to forgo training exercises in Nevada for a real-world op in the Gulf. But they'd stripped equipment already packed, leaving Eleven scrounging and grumbling in their wake.

"With you or me?" He didn't need to ask what Norton was pissed about. Mike had sent his men over to HCS-5 for a little *prowl and growl*. Mission objective: loot a certain case of ouzo. And to make sure Norton thought twice about ever accepting that kind of bribe again, they'd left one bottle with Mike's calling card.

"You."

A smile tugged at the corner of his mouth. "Good."

Keeping that symbiotic relationship between SEALs and Seahawk pilots healthy called for a dose of mischief every once in a while. He'd get back at Hannah for the late bird, as well, but right now he couldn't even stand next to her, without torturing himself with the thought of that big rock on her finger.

She wasn't wearing it. He'd checked.

But that didn't mean Petrone hadn't asked. Or that Hannah hadn't accepted.

She wouldn't wear it at work.

"Not good," she said. "HCS-5 is leaving for the Gulf this morning. Norton's paranoid because your SEALs had free rein around his Seahawks last night. He's quadruple checking everything and holding up our production—"

"You want me to give him a call?"

"No." She checked her watch. "He'll be wheels up in a few. I just wanted to let you know we've been stuck with a C-5 that has a hydraulic leak. It's going to take some time to get it fixed. But I don't want to hold you up."

"Not a problem."

"It's not necessary. We'll see you in Fallon." She started to walk away.

"Time hack," he called her back, before she could disappear. She'd been standing beside him for the past five minutes, keeping a professional distance in everything she said or did. He wanted to break through that. At the very least he wanted her to look at him so he could decide whether those purple smudges underneath her eyes were there because she'd spent the night making love to another man. And the only thing he could think of to get her attention was his watch.

"You call it," she said, fingering the setting on her watch so they could synchronize their time.

Why hadn't he noticed before that it was new? Similar to the one she'd had in Nevada, but new. What was the significance of that?

"Are you going to call it?" she asked.

He stepped in closer, until they were touching. Just a brush of fire-retardant Nomex. But he could feel her heat beneath the flight suit. "0707," he said. "Five, four, three, two, one. Hack." He raised his head. She raised hers. Unhooking her sunglasses from her breast pocket, she put them on. But not before he caught a peek.

She looked tired. Sad.

Did the idea of leaving Petrone cause her that much misery? Or had she caught on to Petrone's game? He hoped it was the latter. But anything out of his own mouth right now would sound like jealous ramblings.

She hitched a ride with the ground crew, leaving

only her scent behind. Women were considered non-combatants, but even he could admit the lines were a little hazy these days and had been since the first Gulf War. Obviously Petrone had never seen Hannah in her element.

Because if he had, he never would have tried to use her as a bargaining chip.

A favor.

Hall-Petrone wanted Lieutenant Commander Stanton as their Navy liaison on the fuel-cell project. If Mike could deliver Hannah, by convincing the admiral, who had already said no—to let her go, Petrone would deliver the fuel cell.

Mike wanted his hands on that fuel cell almost as much as he wanted his hands on Hannah's body. But he respected her too much to touch either. It was her call.

It had always been her call.

"Here," the Senior Chief shoved a clipboard at him, "sign this. The last of the pallets are being loaded now."

Mike scrawled his name to the manifest. "Make sure we have plenty of batteries."

"Will do."

"Tell the men to board. And make sure my Jeep gets onto one of those planes."

With a heavy sigh, Itch shook his head. "Rumor has it the motor pool in Fallon, Nevada, has new Jeeps, some only ten or fifteen years old. Brand spanking new Hummers, too. I bet they'd even let a commander sign for one."

"Now why would I do that when I can bring my own ride along?"

"Oh, I don't know. Maybe because you've been driving around in that same piece of shit since high school."

"Call me sentimental. I keep you around, don't I?"

"I don't recall you having a choice." Though not related by blood, Garret "Itch" Erickson was as close to Mike as any brother. Back in high school Garret had been living out of his car, a car he'd sold off years ago, when Mike's folks had taken him into their foster care. "How are the folks?"

"Should have seen that one coming. I'll call 'em from Fallon," he promised. He'd put off that phone call home too long.

"Did you get the e-mail from Meg, about the anniversary cruise? She wants to book by the end of the month so she can get a good deal. Said she needs the money by then."

"I got it," Mike admitted. "She's being a bit extravagant after last year's bash for their thirty-fifth."

Maureen's husband still wasn't back to driving long haul after his back surgery. Financially, Mary Margaret and her husband were no better off with the new baby, their fourth. And Marla and her husband had been downsized right out of Silicon Valley.

"You know Jenny and I will pitch in," Itch volunteered, despite the fact an enlisted man made much less than an officer.

Mike didn't mind paying the lion's share, but he

knew it put his sisters and their husbands, even Garret in a bind. And who'd take care of Buddy if his folks went off on a second honeymoon? "I just wish Meg would think before she acts."

"Never gonna happen." Itch slapped him on the back, then headed out to issue Mike's orders. "Let's do it!" Itch shouted to the men.

Dawn gave a red-sky warning, highlighting the admiral's words. *Whatever's between the two of you, get it worked out. You have two weeks.* A little hard to do when the whatever was an ache deep in his gut for another man's fiancée.

Do the right thing, Mac.

Mike pushed his sunglasses in place and headed to the last in line of the four-prop C-130 transports.

Doing the right thing might mean stepping aside.

CHAPTER SEVEN

NAVAL AIR STATION FALLON
Fallon, Nevada

"A WORD, COMMANDER." Hannah chose her approach as carefully as if she were landing her Sikorsky HH-60H Seahawk on the rolling and pitching deck of an aircraft carrier.

Flight deck. No cover. No salutes.

No nonsense.

For a moment she thought he didn't hear her above the whirling blades of the second gunship. But when the fully locked and loaded Navy SEAL detached from his squad and executed an about-face it wasn't the landlocked tarmac in the middle of the Nevada desert that lurched.

Hannah stopped short. The thump-thump-thump resonating in her ears could have been the whip of the helicopter's blades or the beat of her own heart. Clutching the crash helmet digging into her hip, she stood her ground, waiting for him to come to her.

He closed the distance with measured strides—a twenty-first-century cowboy headed for a showdown.

"Shoot, Hannah."

Leave it to McCaffrey to be so damn amicable when she wanted nothing more than to shoot him. Too bad her sidearm was loaded with blanks for this training exercise. She would have been satisfied with a flesh wound.

He stopped well out of range of her personal space, crossing well-toned arms to keep her out of his. Over his shoulder, flight crews from the eight gunships of Helicopter Combat Support (Special) Squadron Nine headed back to the hangar not far behind SEAL Team Eleven. Ground crews hovered in the background, sparing them the occasional glance—about as much privacy as they were going to get in full view of their crews.

Brushing wind whipped hair out of her eyes, Hannah tilted her chin. "Do you have a problem with my flying, Commander?"

"Han, we've been over this." He removed his sunglasses, hanging them on his breast pocket. Like the desert-print battle-dress uniform he wore, his hazel eyes provided camouflage, disguising his thoughts as he squinted against the glaring sun to study her face. "Don't take it personally."

"How do you expect me to take it? Your men refuse to get in my gunship."

"Parish is regular, you're reserve. We've established a level of comfort and familiarity with the pilots who actually fly us into combat." His guarded eyes softened as he shifted focus to her mouth, but that softness disappeared an instant later.

Regret?

Damn, it was hot.

Ripping at the Velcro closure of her flight suit, she cleared her throat. "There are eight gunships in this squadron. In the past five days you've flown in seven of them. The majority of those pilots are also reservists. Helicopter Combat Support would not exist without reservists." She knew it. And he knew it. "I'd like to know why I'm the odd man out. Or is *man* the operative word here?"

"It's not because you're a wom—"

She cut him off with a shake of her head. "Keep paying lip service to Navy policy, Commander, then maybe one of us will believe it. I need to maintain combat readiness."

"Hannah, I hope to hell you never see combat." He said it with the authority of a man who'd spent at least part of the past year in a hot zone. He combed a hand through his hair and looked to be about as tired of this conversation as she felt.

"I'm not going to let this go," she warned.

Deal with it. Deal with me.

He scratched at the grit-and-sweat-encrusted five-o'clock shadow that dared to make an early appearance at 1500 hours. His face paint had faded except for a few mud-colored streaks near his hairline.

Even covered in grime, he looked good.

"What do you want me to say?"

She wanted him to admit this wasn't a reserve or gender war; it was something much more personal.

"I want you to say you'll get in my gunship. That's all."

"Okay, Han, tomorrow, I promise I'll get in your gunship."

"Don't patronize me, McCaffrey, tomorrow is Sunday. And I don't know about you, but I'm taking a well-deserved day off. I'm talking about today… this entire past week. You're avoiding me and your men are following your lead."

"I thought we were avoiding each other." His gaze was neither soft nor camouflaged as he forced her to take a hard look at herself. She had been avoiding him. Since she'd walked out on him at lunch, she hadn't said one word to him that didn't have to do with work.

"That's personal. This is professional."

"I see," he said through tight lips.

"You're a SEAL, McCaffrey. You know how to compartmentalize the two."

"You're right, Han, I do. I guess what surprises the hell out of me is that you're so damn good at it."

But she wasn't. Wasn't that the problem? She couldn't separate the personal from the professional. Mike McCaffrey and Commander McCaffrey, Navy SEAL, were one and the same. She just wished she'd realized it sooner.

"You know what? I don't care what it is. I'm CO of this squadron, not Parish. Your guys want a ride next time out, they get in my gunship or else…"

"Or else what?"

She supposed he could have laughed in her face,

a lite commander threatening a full commander, but at this point she was too fed up to care.

"Or else." She brushed past him, knocking into his shoulder on purpose. "That's not a threat, McCaffrey, that's a promise."

Mike turned to watch Hannah walk away. That little knock had been their first physical contact in five days, but he was more than willing to open the door she seemed determined to slam in his face.

Aware of aviation ground crews all around them, he spoke through the Motorola transmitter they used to communicate during ground exercises. "What happened to the ring?"

That brought her up short, though she'd didn't face him.

He knew she wouldn't wear it in the cockpit, but he hadn't seen her wearing it at all since they'd arrived in Fallon. The lingering question had bothered him for days. And just as many sleepless nights.

"It wasn't your ring, McCaffrey. I don't see how it concerns you."

"You don't remember me? Let me refresh your memory. I'm the guy who made you come, not once, not twice, but so many times there weren't enough Trojans lined up to get the job done." The moment he realized he was speaking from the ache in his gut, he knew he'd live to regret his words.

"That's right, McCaffrey, there's no other man that can measure up to you!" She ripped out her earpiece and glared at him over her shoulder. For a split second before she stormed off, he thought he saw her heart in her eyes. Impossible.

Hannah didn't have a heart. She'd proved that by stomping all over his—in size-eight combat boots. But only after he'd been careless with hers. When had they gone from being on the same side to opposing forces? "Suck it up, Mac," he mumbled to himself. "It wasn't personal, it was just sex."

When it came right down to it, all they had was that one night in a hotel room. And he'd sure made a mess out of that.

"Hannah sure has changed." Russell Parish gnawed on a toothpick. He'd shut down his gunship and had come up beside Mike on the tarmac.

"She can still fly circles around any pilot in your squadron. Your time-on-targets need work, Rusty. My men need pilots they can count on."

He favored Parish and some of the other less experienced pilots because they provided more worst-case scenario practice. When Hannah returned to civilian life, Rusty Parish would be the man to take over. He should have mentioned that to Hannah.

She couldn't read his mind.

Mike shook his head, then headed toward the squadron ready room for debriefing. There was a time when he thought she could.

DOUGLAS HOUSE BACHELOR OFFICERS'
QUARTERS
Fallon, Nevada

HANNAH SLUMPED against the door of her room. Mercifully, the debriefing hadn't lasted long. She couldn't do this, not for two weeks, two days, or even two more minutes. The man was insufferable.

Shrugging off the shoulders of her unzipped flight suit, she tied the sleeves around her waist, then she pushed redial on her cell phone and crossed the room to the kitchenette, grabbing a can of something cold out of the refrigerator.

"Hello?" Her sister picked up on the third ring.

"Sammy, it's Han. Did I catch you at a bad time?"

"Hannah, no, the movers just left. We're unpacking. You know Mom, she wanted everything in its proper place right away."

"I told her to leave it. I'll be back in a week. I can unpack then." Hannah paced her small space, feeling helpless. "I feel bad enough making you relocate cross country."

"I'm happy to do it for you and for Fallon. You really didn't expect Mom to leave things alone, did you? Oh, and I should warn you, she's staying."

"What?"

"She's been seeing Captain Loring, though I don't think he's the reason she's decided to stay. Here, I'll let you two duke it out." The phone exchanged hands, and Hannah put on her boxing gloves. Seeing as in dating? Her mother hadn't dated in…her mother had never dated.

"Hannah?"

"Mom, what are you doing? Stop unpacking!"

"Life does not stand still while you're away doing drills or whatever it is you do. Honestly, Hannah, you can't expect us to live like gypsies just because you do."

That was a low blow.

"It's not like I have a choice, Mother."

"Of course you do. You've chosen the glamorous life over family."

"Glamorous?" While her suite at the BOQ was nice, it wasn't exactly Club Med. And she wouldn't call sweating her ass off under the hot desert sun much fun, either. Of course, her mother would never say anything as crass as ass or sweat. A lady never sweated, she perspired. And her mother never even did that. "Try duty, Mother. Maybe you can get the good captain to fill you in on that. Oh!" Hannah exhaled her frustration in one big sigh. "I am so not going to get into this with you. Go home, Mother. Sammy doesn't need a mother hen hanging around. And I don't need you to manage my life."

"You may not need me, Hannah Catherine, but your sister does. She doesn't know the first thing about taking care of a baby—for that matter, neither do you. So I'm here for as long as my granddaughter needs me."

So now her mother had gone from being mopey to feisty?

"Please put Sammy back on the phone."

Hannah knew just as much as any other first-time mother. She'd read the books. She had friends with babies. But more importantly, she loved and missed her daughter. She just couldn't be there. Even though she really wanted to be.

The few minutes Sammy spent reassuring her that the baby was fine didn't make Hannah feel any less restless. When Hannah finally hung up, she felt more frustrated and guilt ridden than ever.

BASE COMMISSARY
Fallon, Nevada

HANNAH HAD TO BREAK OUT of the sweltering confines of her room, so she headed to the Navy commissary, where the air-conditioning was actually working. She didn't even bother to change out of her flight suit.

Being Saturday, the store was crowded with service members in uniform and civilian clothes, retirees and their spouses, and military wives pushing cartloads of groceries and children. The one-way aisles gave the commissary a military efficiency unlike any civilian grocery store. And she was able to skip through until she hit the meat department. Low prices were a benefit and a curse.

She was waiting for the butcher to restock the porterhouse steaks when she realized someone had dropped a couple of T-bones in her cart by mistake. She looked around expecting to find a stranger searching for his missing meat. Instead she found McCaffrey dumping produce into her cart. Prepackaged salad. Potatoes. "What are you doing?"

"Shadowing you."

"Some might call that stalking."

He'd showered and changed into blue jeans and a denim shirt since their debriefing. Not one to waste a minute, his hair was still damp. "I'm trying to apologize. I tried to get your attention after debriefing, and again in the parking lot. I suppose you didn't hear me call your name."

"No, sorry, I didn't." They both knew she was lying. "Unless you were that guy in the beat-up orange Jeep trying to run me down."

"I missed you by a mile."

They'd moved on from the meat department, with McCaffrey steering the cart. She noticed that he'd shaved. Although she knew he used unscented products, he still had a fresh, clean scent about him, a combination of a hot summer breeze, warm skin and cool surf—even though they were miles away from a body of water.

She felt grimy just standing next to him.

Saturday night. Shower. He was probably headed out to one of the many clubs on and off base.

"Get your own cart," she said, as he continued to fill hers.

"They're all out up front."

"I'm trying to keep my number of items down so I can go through the express lane."

"We'll split up when we get to the checkout," he said.

"I hate when people do that. That's cheating."

"How is that cheating?"

"If you're in such a hurry to hit the town tonight, you shouldn't even be shopping. You knew it was going to be crowded."

A hint of amusement shone in his eyes. She was avoiding his apology like she'd been avoiding him all week. And he knew it. Or at least suspected it.

"Truce?" he asked.

She was mad at him and she wanted to stay mad at him, but the truth was she was so tired of fighting with him, and her mother, that his over-the-top charm presented the perfect foil for her bad mood. She cracked a smile. "I'll think about it."

That is, until she saw what he was contemplating in the drug aisle. Did he think he was just going to sneak condoms by her? Three packs? Extra large. Especially when he wasn't hitting on her.

She'd realized he'd probably enjoyed sex in the past year, but she hadn't thought about it until now. Her stomach knotted and nothing in the cart looked appetizing anymore.

"Let me get your expert opinion," he asked. "What do women really want? Ribbed for her pleasure or extra lubricated?" He held up the two packages. "I always wanted to ask that without getting arrested."

"Try the ones that glow in the dark," she said, choosing the least appealing. Except maybe whatever bimbo he picked up would think that fun. "And skip the lubricant."

"Really?"

"Uh-huh," she agreed. She even managed to keep a straight face as she reached past him for a box of tampons, hoping to humiliate him into finding his own cart.

But her choice of weapons backfired. She hadn't had her period since giving birth to Fallon, which only served to remind her that they'd made a baby together. And he was sleeping with other women. She threw a couple more feminine hygiene products into the cart without even looking at them.

"Is that it?" she asked. "I think I'm at my limit for the express lane."

"No, that's not it." He took out his list and turned down the next aisle. "Peanut butter?" he asked, picking up the Peter Pan.

"I like this brand better." She reached around him for the Smuckers All Natural and a jar of Strawberry Simply Fruit, and set them in the cart. He tossed the Peter Pan in anyway.

The aisle ahead was blocked by a young mother who struggled to keep an infant and two small boys under control.

"They never had shopping carts like that when I was a kid." Mac eyed the big plastic truck with envy.

"You can see why."

The woman was having a hard time keeping her boys from escaping the side doors, and at the same time keeping them separated so they would quit pounding on each other. The infant in the Snugli cried as the woman scolded the boys. When she stopped to comfort the baby, the boys opened the doors to the plastic truck and made good their escape.

Against traffic, they wove in and out of shoppers, racing and laughing in the face of their mother's distress.

"Whoa, there!" McCaffrey swept up a boy in each arm. "Where do you two think you're going?" he asked in a voice that could reverse the potty training of grown men. "Turn around and march back to your mother."

Neither boy moved.

"That's an order."

The youngest took his cue from his older brother and they both gave a pretty good imitation of stiff-legged toy soldiers. Hannah hid her smile behind her hand.

Mac followed not too far behind the boys, and Hannah, with the cart, covered his rear, trying not to notice how nice it was.

"Thank you kindly," the flustered and very pregnant young mother said. Hannah longed to reach out and stroke her baby's dark head. "We just came from seein' their daddy off." Cart loaded with comfort food, she struggled to hold back tears. "I promised these two a treat if they could behave themselves." Her scowl showed her displeasure.

"Tell you what," Mac said, hunkering down to their level. He pulled his wallet from his back pocket. "This one's on me." He held out a five-dollar bill toward the oldest boy. When the boy went to take it, McCaffrey snatched it back. "If you can behave."

The boy nodded, eager for his reward.

"While your daddy's gone, he wouldn't want you misbehaving for your momma now, would he? No," Mac answered for the little boy, shaking his head. "Here you go." He handed over the bribe. "I suppose you want one, too," he asked the younger brother.

The boy nodded.

Mac handed over another five. "Don't spend it all in one place."

"What do you boys say?" the mother prompted.

"Thank you, sir," they spoke in unison.

"You're welcome. Remember what I said." He pushed to his feet, and Hannah stole one last look at the baby.

"Bribery," she said as they moved ahead of the family to finish their shopping. "Now there's a parenting skill that comes in handy."

"You have a better way?"

"Well, I wouldn't bribe my kids."

"If they were mine, I would have turned them over my knee."

"I can't believe you condone spanking."

"A little punishment and reward go a long way."

"So basically, if your children were upset because their father had deployed, you'd treat them like prisoners of war?"

"First of all, if these hypothetical children were upset because their father left, then I wouldn't be there, would I? So it would be my wife who had to deal with it and not me."

"So when you're not spanking your kids you're leaving all the responsibility of discipline to your wife?"

He raised his hands in surrender. "I don't have any, I don't want any. And I sure as hell don't want a wife. So what does it matter?" He grinned at her. "I'm not turning anybody over my knee unless you continue with this line of questioning, Commander."

That earned him a wink from the retired gentleman in front of them when they pulled into the long checkout line. But the old gent was wise enough to keep any comments to himself. And nosy enough to check out the items in their basket. Aside from junk, like peanut butter and crackers, they had the makings of an intimate dinner for two. And then some.

Hannah lowered her voice. "Did your father spank you?"

"You're kidding, right? My dad was a long-haul trucker, he was never home. And when he was, he never raised a hand to any of us."

"Your mother?"

"Nooo." He dragged out the single syllable. "She disciplined with a look—" he demonstrated "—and the wait-till-your-father-gets-home threat. But thank you for being so concerned about my welfare. I suppose you're going to raise brats with 'time outs' and 'boundaries.'" He supplied the air quotes.

"Of course. Only my kids won't be *brats*," she said, taking offense at his comment.

"Good luck with that. It's easy to see you're from a small family. There are no boundaries after the third kid. Take those two boys and the pregnant stressed-out mom carrying a baby, double that, and you have some idea of what it was like to grow up in my family."

Six kids? Eight kids? How many kids were in his family? Terror must have shown on her face, because he seemed all the more amused by it. "I guess it's a good thing those brats of yours are hypothetical," she snapped.

CHAPTER EIGHT

DOUGLAS HOUSE BACHELOR OFFICERS' QUARTERS
Fallon, Nevada

BY SOME UNSPOKEN AGREEMENT Mike got stuck with kitchen duty while Hannah showered and changed out of her uniform. He had steaks grilling on the hibachi outside, potatoes baking in the microwave and vegetables sautéing on the stove by the time he heard the shower shut off.

He really had tracked her down at the commissary to apologize. But the dinner invitation had been inspired. He'd just kept piling items into her cart. Then he'd given her a ride back to the BOQ. And since his room was right across from hers, there was no reason for him not to help carry her groceries…

It all felt a little underhanded on his part, but they really did need to stop avoiding each other.

Moving between the kitchen and the small patio in his Kiss The Cook apron, he felt more relaxed than he'd remembered being in a long time—until Hannah emerged from the bathroom. Mike could almost convince himself that someone who looked that hot in a white tank top and blue jeans with strategic rips didn't care about a big bank account.

She never wore makeup in the field. But tonight she'd added a hint of natural color to her lips that he wanted to kiss off. She had that homey, comfortable look as she padded around him in her bare feet. "How is it you know how to cook?"

"How is it you don't?" He stopped long enough to hand her the bottle of ouzo he'd brought over from his room. "Make yourself useful and pour," he teased.

"Where did you get this?" She reached for two glasses above the sink.

"I have a whole case, compliments of HCS-5."

"Guess I owe you an apology for that." She poured two fingers in each glass and handed one to him.

"I'm the one who was out of line today. You were right to call me on it. I can't turn back the clock and change things I've said and done to hurt you, Han. I'm not sure I would, even if I could. I'm not sorry for those things, only sorry that I've made such a big mess of them."

"To no apologies, and no excuses," she said, clinking their glasses.

He slammed back the ouzo.

The anise-flavored liquor cleansed his pallet, but not his culpability. "I'd like to drink to *homonoia*," he said, measuring out two more shots. "Greek's a little rusty, but it means oneness of mind."

"I'll drink to that, though Alcibiades and Socrates argued that men and women couldn't live in agreement. *Homonoia* described the male bond. So to hell with ancient scholars." She raised her glass. "What do they know?"

He leaned back against the counter. "What's the word for the male/female bond?"

"*Homophrosune.* It means oneness of heart." Blushing, she raised her glass to her lips.

Oneness of heart. And oneness of mind.

He'd drink to that.

"You didn't answer my question about cooking," she said, and the moment for oneness was gone.

"Bachelor training," he said, while hanging up his apron. His own father had been a stable influence despite his long absences. But the responsibility of a big family, which included a child with special needs, required sacrifices Mike was unwilling to make. Selfish, maybe. Realistic, yes. Especially in his line of work.

"Let me guess. First lesson, the art of seduction."

"Starvation. Learn how to cook or starve."

"I don't know if I believe you. I'll bet you know plenty of women who'd cook for you." She picked up two plastic wineglasses in her free hand and grabbed a bottle of wine from the refrigerator, then led the way out to the patio where he'd set their table.

"One or two," he answered modestly. That was not the conversation he wanted to have with her.

The seat of her jeans fit snugly across her curved

bottom. Oh, baby. And him with only four packs of condoms.

She sat down, tucking one foot under her other leg.

"Your turn," he said.

She poured the wine while he tended the grill and fixed their plates. "Never all that interested in cooking. I like eating though," she said, taking a bite of a sautéed green pepper. "I remember wanting an Easy Bake oven. I must have been seven."

He served, then joined her at the table. "My sisters had one of those. You didn't?"

She shook her head and took another swallow. "Didn't have a birthday that year."

"Why not?" he asked, settling in for the conversation.

She studied a crack in the stem of her plastic wineglass. They'd picked up the glasses at the package store along with the wine.

"That was the year my father died. We had a funeral instead. I don't think anyone even remembered it was my birthday. Anyway, it was a long time ago."

They drank in silence for a while. Her father had died while doing what Mike loved. Those things would always be there. Which was why he wasn't even in the running with Petrone.

"Your birthday's coming up, isn't it?"

"I guess I get a little morbid around my birthday. But let me give you a hint, women don't like to talk about getting older," she said, steering him clear of the subject.

He liked listening to her talk about herself, and even though she shied away from intimate details, he encouraged her to keep talking so he could keep listening. The fire in her sultry voice made the arid desert night crackle.

She told him about her college days, where she'd met Petrone. About joining the Navy, flight school, helicopters, about hitting the glass ceiling that kept her subordinate to the men in her unit and how she finally broke free as a civilian only to take up the challenge of switching from being a conventional pilot to a special warfare pilot as a reservist. "I thought if it was going to be that hard for me as a woman, I might as well make it even harder on myself. I was surprised to get the command nod though," she admitted, glancing down at the remains on her plate and pushing it aside before meeting his gaze.

"You deserve it, Han," he said with all sincerity. "You're the best damn pilot out there, today and every day."

"I don't know if everyone would agree with you on that. But you're right, I deserve it. It almost makes me wish I'd stayed active duty…because here I am." She raised her hands in surrender. *"Almost,"* she emphasized. "Not quite."

"Can't wait to get back to your civilian life?"

"Aren't you sick of hearing me talk about myself? Tell me what it was like growing up in a big family?"

He picked up the quarter he'd been playing with

on and off all night and gave her the rundown on all his sisters while skirting the issue of Buddy's disability. She wasn't the only one shying away from intimate details.

The candle burned low in his makeshift wine bottle candlestick holder, and though he thought the air-conditioning in the building had come back on, they continued to hang out on the patio.

He filtered out the background noise of a Saturday night at the BOQ with residents coming and going. Lights from their building and others flickered on and off around them.

It took him a full minute to realize neither of them had said a word in some time. She was intent on watching his hand as he rolled the quarter over and under his fingers. "Want to give it a try?"

"I don't think I can."

He took her left hand in his. "It's a good exercise in dexterity for your nondominant hand." He placed the quarter on her knuckles between two of her fingers. "Raise this one, lower that one. Raise, lower, flip."

"Like that's so easy." She laughed at her attempt.

He kept her at it, and before too long she had the hang of it. Technically, she was holding the quarter and he was holding her hand. But when he brushed his thumb across her ring finger, she turned her hand and touched him. And they were holding hands across the table.

"Petrone's a lucky guy," he said, thinking it was

time for him to call it a night. But instead of letting her go, he tugged her hand and guided her around the table and into his lap.

She cradled his face, brought her mouth to his and kissed him. Sweet, soft, openmouthed kisses that held the fruity taste of wine, the spicy taste of ouzo and another drug beside the alcohol that could only be called desire.

She took him deeper into addiction with her tongue.

Blood rushed from his brain. His last coherent thought was that Petrone's luck had just run out. His groin grew heavy, then hard against the curve of her hip, aching to mimic the play of their tongues.

"I want you," he murmured against her lips, so there would be no mistaking where he wanted to go.

HANNAH REACHED UP and turned on the bedside lamp.

McCaffrey's weight shifted on the bed behind her. "*Now* you want the light on," he said in a groggy voice. "It's two in the morning, Han. Go back to sleep." He reached up and turned the light off.

"I think you should leave." She turned it back on.

He propped himself up on his elbows. "I'm staying."

"Somebody might see you."

"This isn't a boot camp, Han. Nobody is coming around to do a bed check. I'll leave in the morning. And no one will see me, I promise." He reached around her and turned off the light. This time his arm came around her and he snuggled up to her backside.

How had they gone from holding hands to ripping off each other's clothes? She couldn't even claim she'd had too much to drink because she hadn't lost consciousness, only her conscience. What was she thinking?

She slipped out from under his arm. Putting on her tank top and her boy-cut briefs, she slipped into the bathroom and turned on the light.

She couldn't even face herself in the mirror. She fumbled around in the medicine cabinet while she filled a glass of water. After taking the pills, she felt some of the tension leave her body. She squeezed toothpaste on her toothbrush and began brushing her teeth.

"Should I be insulted that you're in here scrubbing your mouth out after kissing me?" McCaffrey asked, leaning against the doorjamb.

"I always brush my teeth before bed."

Kiss didn't even begin to describe the intimacy. She'd kissed him, yes. But she'd also taken him deep into her mouth, kneeling before him as if he were some sort of demigod, and she his willing slave.

He stepped into the bathroom. Naked. A fully locked and loaded Navy SEAL with a hard-on.

She rinsed her mouth. And tried to keep her eyes in her head where they belonged. He borrowed her toothbrush. While brushing his teeth, he read the package for the pills she'd taken. "What's the deal?" he asked when he finished. "Why emergency contraceptives?"

How could she explain? She was *that* afraid of another pregnancy. They were already bound by a child she loved, but hadn't told him about. "You said it had been a while, I just had an uneasy feeling," she admitted.

Actually, he had said... *"Stop torturing me with that mouth of yours. I don't know if I can hold out much longer. It's been a while...since us."*

Since us. And she was lost.

She'd sheathed him in that Day-Glo condom. They'd had a good laugh over how much it looked like the green glow sticks the SEALs strapped to armbands when swimming at night. Then she'd straddled him and confessed, *"Since us. I haven't been with another man, Mike." And when she whispered, "I'm not going to marry Peter. I never was," Mike didn't hold out on her any longer.*

"Come here," he said, pulling her to him. "I wore a condom. You're wearing a birth-control patch." He sneaked a hand under the hem of her tank top and brushed his thumb along the evidence at her hip. "We're safe. How about we take a shower together and scrub some other body cavities?" he teased.

He pushed her briefs down her hips and she tugged them back up. "Let me light a candle."

"Again with the lights?" But he turned them off. The soft glow of candlelight surrounded them as he turned on the shower.

The darkness hid the changes in her body that

she didn't want him to see. But she couldn't hide from the shame she felt for not telling Mike about Fallon as she made love to her baby's father for a second time that night.

> ACTIVITY FOR THE DAY. SATURDAY AND SUNDAY. TAKE ONE DAY OFF AND USE THE OTHER DAY FOR ENDURANCE TRAINING ACCORDING TO YOUR PREFERENCES. ALL PERSONNEL. UNIFORM: CIVILIAN CASUAL. REQ SOPA ADMIN PASS TO HCS-9 AND ST-11.

HANNAH RIPPED the memo from the bulletin board. According to her preference, last night qualified as endurance training. She didn't need to beat herself up about it any more than she already had.

She thrived on routine. Sunday had always been her day to catch up on laundry for the coming work week. She entered the laundry room juggling an overstuffed collapsible hamper and laundry supplies to find two of the dryers stopped with the BDUs just sitting there getting wrinkled. Why was it men never stuck around long enough to tend to their clothes? Or anything else for that matter? That wasn't really fair—McCaffrey had left her bed early this morning at her request.

As for the washing machines, she opened lid after lid only to see that all but one of them was full. Damned if she'd wait around all day for the owner or owners of the uniforms to come back. She opened the finished dryers with the intention of unloading them, so she had some place to put the washed clothes. But after she did that and started her first load, her type A personality took over and she started folding cammies and stacking them neatly in a pile.

McCaffrey walked in carrying a box of laundry detergent. "If I'd known you were so domestic I'd have proposed long before Petrone."

"And what would you have proposed? That we shack up so I could do your laundry? I think I'll pass. I take it this is yours." She finished folding a green T-shirt and set it on top of the growing pile.

He picked up another and started folding along-side her. "Are you sure? Because I could really use a laundress. I could see some fringe benefits."

"I'm sure you could. Unfortunately I can't see any for me."

"Can't picture yourself in a lacy little apron? Me chasing you around the house?"

"A, you'd never be home. And B, you'd never catch me in an apron, cute or otherwise. The domes-tic-goddess fantasy is a guy thing."

"You're forgetting I can cook. What if I put on the apron?" He lifted a suggestive brow.

"Now that would be something to see."

"So did I have all the machines tied up, is that what you're complaining about?"

"Yes."

"Ran out of soap. Got some whites in the washer

ready to go. Not a full load if you have something you want to toss in."

"It wasn't this machine, was it? She lifted the lid and dug up a pair of his wet briefs. "Am I as pink as these, do you think? I'm sorry—" she tried not to crack a smile "—I didn't see anything in there."

He sighed heavily. "Guess I need to head back to the Navy Exchange for some bleach, or the whole men's locker room will be laughing at me. Since it looks like we're going to be here a while, why don't I grab a pizza from the food court?"

"Sounds good. I have some bleach, but I don't think it's going to do the trick. You might want to buy yourself some new underwear. There's a twenty in my purse—"

"I'll collect later," he said, his voice husky enough to leave no doubt what kind of exchange he had in mind.

The moment he'd walked in, she knew she was going to sleep with him again. Not sleep with. Have sex with.

She was going to have sex with him again, and again, and again…until she got him out of her system. After all it had been a while for her, too. *Since us.*

As a pregnant singleton, and now a single mom, she didn't have that many opportunities to date. She was going to take full advantage of this situation. There, she'd thought it, she could do it. She could have sex. Sex and nothing more. With McCaffrey.

While he went for underwear and pizza, Hannah

started more laundry and settled in with the latest Stephen Coonts novel. Funny McCaffrey didn't seem the type to harbor domestic fantasies. Certainly not the kind that required setting up housekeeping with someone. But the man could cook. And he did his own laundry. Though she'd have to be living a complete fantasy to ever think that the two—or rather the three—of them could build a home together.

McCaffrey returned a half hour later carrying a pizza box and a six-pack of bottled beer he'd said he'd had in his room.

She greedily took a slice of cheese pizza before he even had the chance to put it down. She might regret the carbs later, but they'd sure taste good going down.

"Anything mysterious happen to my clothes while I was gone?"

"Other than them getting up and walking out, no," she said around a bite.

"Seriously, they're not going anywhere. There's a game I want to watch. Diamondbacks and Rockies. We could eat this in your room," he suggested.

She cast him a look. She knew what was on his mind.

"What? I don't bite."

"As I recall, you do," she said, pushing to her feet to lead the way back to her room. "I'm kicking you out at 2200 hours. You're sleeping in your own bed tonight."

"That gives us all afternoon, and evening."

And he'd left his Kiss The Cook apron in her kitchen.

CHAPTER NINE

THE NAVY DAY STARTED at the crack of dawn. A mother's day started even earlier. Since giving birth, 0400 had been the norm. Hannah shuffled to the bathroom in the dark, pulling a white tank top over her sport bra and cutoff gray sweats. McCaffrey, moving around in her kitchenette by the soft glow of refrigerator light, registered only after the shock of cold water hit her face.

A moment later she emerged from the bathroom finger-combing her hair.

"Mornin'. Coffee?" He took a sip and handed her the cup without waiting for her answer. "Cream and sugar, just the way you like it."

Now how had he remembered that? Her own head was a bit fuzzy this morning. She hadn't slept well after she'd kicked him out of her bed. "How'd you get in?"

He held up a key card. "I took your spare."

He had a key. What did she care? He wasn't going to steal anything, except maybe her heart. But only if she let him. And she wasn't going to let him. Good in bed didn't translate to permanent fixture in her life. As long as she remembered that their daughter was a beautiful gift, not his shackle—she'd be fine.

She took her first sip. The intimacy of the morning-coffee ritual seemed all too natural. "Thank you."

"You're welcome."

Polite, awkward intimacy.

He poured himself a cup.

Maybe not so awkward. He leaned back against the counter to drink, looking adorably rumpled in his T-shirt and running shorts. Had he slept in them? "Ready?" he asked, setting his cup aside after a few minutes.

"Not really, but yes." Out of habit, she strapped on the fanny pack that held her ID and pepper spray, though probably not a precaution she needed when going out for a morning jog with a Navy SEAL escort.

They warmed up in the predawn light by walking at a brisk pace to the trailhead, then stretched before taking off as if this had been their routine for months.

"What's on your agenda for the day?" he asked, pulling up beside her after he'd dropped behind to let a jogger headed in the opposite direction pass. Everyone wanted to get in their run before the heat of the day. Though it wasn't exactly crowded at oh, dark-thirty.

"Morning PT. Morning muster. A pit stop at the motor pool. Meeting with SEAL Team CO…" She eyed him with suspicion. "You didn't get the chance to look over this week's agenda yet, did you?"

"I looked it over and tossed it out."

"What about the training scenarios?"

"What about 'em?"

"Loring—"

"Was your predecessor. And my training philosophy is different than that of Team One."

"Those scenarios weren't all that different from what we've done in the past when Nine and Eleven trained together."

"That's because, as I said, Loring's training philosophy was different than mine. He outranked me, and I had to compromise."

"And you outrank me, so you expect me to do all the compromising? Ow!" She stumbled on a loose pebble. She steadied herself, but he caught her by the arm.

"I thought we'd reach our own compromise." He held both her arm and her gaze long enough for her to feel the electric undercurrents before he let go.

She picked up her pace, staring straight at the sun coming up over the next rise. "What do you have in mind?"

"A more integrated approach between your squadron and my team. Ratchet up the competition level and the fun factor. And then there's the little matter of a side bet between the COs."

"Uh-huh." They'd barely covered a mile, let alone the three they'd agreed on. Her breathing had become more labored while she tried to keep up with McCaffrey's pace. So she stopped to confront him on his *little matter.* Every year the two units ended their two weeks training together with a picnic, the highlight of which was the tug-of-war—SEALs dragging Aviators through mud to collect money for charity.

"What's the bet?" Suspicion crept into her voice.

"A kayaking trip. Six days. Six nights. Just you, me and Itch as chaperone. We need a female to round out our team to raise money for the Warrior Foundation."

The Special Operations Warrior Foundation was there to help the families of fallen SpecWar soldiers and had paid for her and her sister's college education. How could she say no? Still she hesitated.

"It's not like Uncle Sam is giving out leave right now. Besides, I don't know anything about kayaking and it's still a sucker bet. Your guys always win. I may as well hand over my per diem to the Warrior Foundation right now."

"Is that a no, you won't accept the challenge? Or a no, you're afraid to accept the challenge? Uncle Sam's not going to object. It's for a worthy cause. And it's a fair bet. This year it's not going to be Warriors against Wings." They started running again as he laid out his objectives for the next week. "We work together as if this were the real thing."

ACTIVITY OF THE DAY. 0430 TUESDAY. PT/1.5 MILE SWIM/STRETCH. ALL PERSONNEL. UNIFORM: APPROPRIATE

WORKOUT ATTIRE. REQ SOPA ADMIN
PASS TO HCS-9 AND ST-11.

THEY'D HASHED OUT the details for a new training
schedule over dinner at her kitchen counter. By the
time the squadron mustered in their assigned hangar
bay for morning PT on Tuesday, she stood before
them with a new agenda. "At ease," she ordered.

"Monday," Russ Parish read the PT schedule over
her shoulder. "Stretch, obstacle course, three-mile
run, stretch. Boy, I'm glad it's not Monday. Tuesday
PT, one-point-five mile swim, stretch—"

Hannah brought the clipboard to her chest so
he'd stop.

"Sounds like the Navy SEAL Physical Fitness
Program," Chief Webb Emerson said, right on the
money.

"It is," she confirmed. "Petty Officer Bell, front
and center, please," she called the young woman out
of formation. "You're our new physical fitness coor-
dinator." She handed Bell the clipboard. "From now
on, morning muster for PT is 0430." She raised her
voice enough to get the requisite collective groan
from the squadron.

"So if we're clear on the agenda," Hannah said.
"Petty Officer Bell will take it from here. Libby…"
Hannah handed over her squadron to the younger
woman. The admiral's daughter was an exotic beauty
like her mother. It might be hard for the frogs to
imagine the five-foot-two rescue swimmer pulling

anyone out of the water, let alone a six-feet-two pack-weighted Navy SEAL, but Hannah knew all about that kind of drive and determination.

Hannah had already run three miles with McCaffrey for her own PT. And she'd stretch in her room tonight. She'd skip the swim to get some of her other responsibilities out of the way. Besides, it would give her the perfect opportunity to call home. Without Mac around.

ACTIVITY FOR THE DAY. 0430 WEDNESDAY. PT/4-5 MILE RUN WITH FARTLEK WORKOUT/STRETCH. ALL PERSONNEL. UNIFORM: APPROPRIATE WORKOUT ATTIRE. REQ SOPA ADMIN PASS TO HCS-9 AND ST-11.

LONG AFTER THEIR scheduled workout, Mike found Hannah in the gym. He leaned against the wall watching her rapid-fire assault on a poor defenseless punching bag. "Bell might be taking her duties a bit too seriously."

"She's just enthusiastic."

"But you're not helping your teammates any by skipping out on swimming." That got her attention.

She stopped punching. But only long enough to move on to the big bag.

"Bell sent me a memo," he said.

"I had to stop by the motor pool. And used the opportunity to call home. It's not like we don't have a full day of training in the Seahawks, even with the stepped-up workout schedule." Putting all her weight behind one punch, she got the bag to swing. She skipped back a few steps so it wouldn't catch her on the rebound.

Mike held it in place so she could take a few more jabs. "I have the Jeep."

"We're not connected at the hip, McCaffrey. There are places I *need* to go without you."

He noticed she didn't say *want.*

"So take the keys. You have my permission."

"Too late. I already signed for a vehicle. What else did Bell say in her memo?"

"She didn't say anything else. But it sounds like you're ready for a little hand-to-hand combat." He didn't know what the deal was—only that Hannah got worked up every time she called home.

"Are you?" she asked in a breathy voice, hitting the bag one final time.

He grunted with satisfaction when he felt it in his gut.

She gave him a smug look and turned to reach for her water bottle. Beads of sweat trickled between her shoulder blades and stained the gray sports bra. The cutoff sweats hugged her ass as she bent over. It was hard to keep his mind on work all day when he had *that* waiting for him at night. "Ready for anything, that's my motto," he said.

She held the sports bottle between gloved fists and took a sip. "Ready to get in the ring?"

"You'd love taking a couple pokes at me, wouldn't you? Wouldn't be fair, I wouldn't hit back."

"I take it your mother never taught you about girls like me." She pulled at the lace of her boxing glove with her teeth.

He took over the task of unlacing, surprised that she'd even let him. "Mom never did. But Dad saw to it that my education wasn't lacking," he teased. "From the time I was thirteen 'no hitting your sisters' was rule number one in the McCaffrey house. I got in a few licks before then, though."

"How many?"

He looked up from pulling off the first glove. "Licks?" he asked, tucking the glove under his arm.

"No silly. Sisters. How many sisters did you grow up with? It was hard to keep track with all those M names."

"Four sisters. One brother."

She studied him carefully. "Six. You're the oldest," she made the bold assumption a statement and not a question.

"Unless you count Itch, who moved in with us when I was fifteen and he was sixteen, I'm the oldest," he confirmed with a crooked grin, starting on the other glove.

"It shows. You think you know everything." She took him down to the mat with lightning speed. The glove under his arm bounced across the floor. The other wound up above his head when she pinned his wrists.

"I know enough to let you take me down."

She pushed to her knees. "Let me? This isn't the

WWE. I took you by surprise, McCaffrey." She sure as hell had, starting with last Saturday night.

He couldn't have kept the grin off his face if he tried.

"You can take me any way you want me, Stanton." He rolled her beneath him.

She freed herself. He pinned her again.

"Now what are you going to do?" He held her down long enough so he could catch his own breath.

"I've dealt with my share of creeps, especially when I was a junior officer."

"Just give me names," he said. And meant it.

"Oh, I've since learned how to wither a man with just a look." She gave him a demonstration that ended with him shaking his head—the look was too damn sexy to wither any man.

"You two rewriting the Kamasutra, or is that some new form of Tai Chi?" Itch asked.

Mike got to his feet and held out his hand to Hannah. She ignored his offer and helped herself to her feet. "We were debating which is the weaker sex," Mike said. "What do you think, Chief?"

"That's easy. Man."

Hannah raised an I-told-you-so brow.

"You're a big help," Mike said to the Chief. "I forget you crossed over to the dark side."

ACTIVITY FOR THE DAY. 0430 THURS-DAY. RUN 3 MILES/SWIM 1/RUN 3/STRETCH. ALL PERSONNEL. UNI-

FORM: APPROPRIATE WORKOUT AT-
TIRE & GEAR. REQ SOPA ADMIN PASS
TO HCS-9 AND ST-11.

AFTER THEIR FINAL morning run and stretch of the day,
Hannah had headed over to the firing range for extra
points and to update her quals with a handgun. She'd
missed swimming again. For the same reasons as last
time. A phone call home. A few stolen moments with
her computer and the baby cam. And because she
didn't want to fall apart in front of her squadron. Anytime she got near the water, that was a possibility.

Taking out her frustration on a paper target
seemed an appropriate alternative. Between the ear-
muffs, the safety goggles and the other shooters firing off rounds, she didn't hear McCaffrey approach
her from behind. But she could feel him. She took
aim at the target and fired several rounds.

"A little low," he said.

"Maybe it's the distraction." She took off the ear-
muffs and looked at him over her shoulder. "Or
maybe I was just aiming low." She put the muffs back
on and willed him away. When that didn't work, she
became blunt. "Go away."

Every morning at 0400 on the dot, he handed her
a cup of coffee after first taking a sip. It hadn't bothered her at first, now it did. Because every night she
fell asleep in his arms and every morning she woke
up alone. Her choice, she reminded herself.

"Still low. It's your aim." He pushed a button.

The target zipped forward. He snatched it down, pointing out the cluster of low shots. "Ouch. Hit the vitals, at least. If you didn't kill him, you'd sure as hell piss him off."

"Are you finished?" She ripped the target from his grasp, put a new one on the hanger, then sent it speeding back one hundred yards. "I'm a little rusty, that's all. I'm not a pistol-packing mama in my civilian life...." She trailed off, realizing what she'd just said.

"Well, you're no longer a civilian, Commander. Two middle mass, for an easy target." He demonstrated with his own gun. "Two to the head, if you really want to get the job done. But the head's not for amateurs. Think you can handle it?"

He launched a clean target. And handed her his weapon. A Glock 9mm. She took aim, both hands on the weapon, finger on the trigger. Her comment had gone right over his head. But how many slipups were going to get by him before he caught on?

"Feet farther apart." He kicked at her boots, his leg snuggled between her open thighs. "Knees slightly bent." He nudged her.

His hand on her hip was impersonal. Instructive. But it was enough to bother her. "Are we doing the tango here? Or am I taking a shot at the target?"

He removed his hand. "Take the shot."

She took aim.

"Two middle mass."

She fired.

"Higher. Two more middle mass. That's it. Again."

She fired.

"Again. Head. Heart. Head again," he said.

She fired on target. The weapon in her hand became an extension of her arm.

"Heart. You don't just want to stop this guy. Head. You want to kill him. Always shoot to kill. It's kill or be killed."

When she ran out of ammo, she set the weapon down and he brought in her target. The best she'd ever done. "Not bad. What do you think?" she asked a short time later with her expert certificate in hand.

"I think it's easy to shoot up a piece of paper. Try it when the guy is looking you in the eye," he said, clearly not impressed. "You want to walk thorough the pop-ups or head over to the pool?"

Hannah chose urban combat drills over freestyle swimming. They went in as partners with their HK MP-5s. McCaffrey instructed her in high, low, left, right sweeps and leapfrog. She peered around corners before running across streets, clinging to buildings as he instructed.

They traded hand signals. Eyes on target. Eyes on me. Follow me. Wait for my signal. Halt. They worked their way through the maze as if they'd been working together for years. Because, of course, they had.

She fired at a pop-up of a bad guy. Skipped around the pop-up of an old woman carrying a bag of groceries. And froze in a standoff with a Tango taking a child hostage. Tango the code word for the letter *T*, which in this case stood for the big *T*—terrorist.

Mac covered for her, shooting the bad guy right between the eyes.

"What the hell, Stanton." McCaffrey chewed her ass
for that—no less than she expected or deserved. They'd
spent a near perfect week working together. Falling
back into old patterns, perhaps with a new awareness.
"About what I said earlier," he clarified, "never look
the guy in the eye, or stop to think about the shot. The
bad guy's a target. Nothing more. Nothing less."

TRAINING POOL
Fallon, Nevada

FROM THE OBSERVATION DECK, Mike witnessed the silent splash as Hannah entered the water. Clouds of
oxygen bubbles surrounded the swimmer, then
floated to the surface as she frog-kicked through them.
She swam the entire length of the pool underwater.

"I'll be damned. Calypso."

What in the hell was she doing here this late at
night?

And alone?

She surfaced at the opposite end. Covered in man-
nish swim trunks and the top of a tropical swimsuit,
she bobbed for a moment before kicking off to skim
the surface freestyle.

Mike scrambled to the scaffolding that made up
the upper observation deck. Leaning against the rail,
he watched and waited in silence.

The building that housed their Olympic-size pool

had been locked down for hours. Every SEAL knew better than to swim without a buddy. She hadn't even bothered to turn on any other lights. She had a thing about the dark these days.

The sea nymph finished her laps. She crawled out of the pool and picked up her towel.

"I didn't even know you could swim." His voice easily carried to her.

She looked up in his direction. He moved from the shadows. The gangway on his left took him to the pool area and he followed the stairs down.

"How long have you been here?" she asked, continuing to pat herself dry.

He strode toward her. "Long enough."

"I suppose you're going to lecture me for swimming without a buddy."

"I thought you'd forgotten how. I see now that you've just forgotten the rules."

She tossed her towel to the bleachers. "I know how to swim, McCaffrey. Every Navy pilot has to be a First Class qualified swimmer."

The test wasn't as tough as the Navy SEAL swim test, but it wasn't a cakewalk, either, he'd give her that. Still... "That's no excuse for swimming alone."

"I know you're right. That doesn't mean I like it," she admitted, sitting down on the edge and dipping her feet into the pool.

He joined her there, still in his own swimwear. "You don't have to like it. You just have to obey it.

It's the first rule of common sense, and one every BUD/S learns the first day of training."

She stared at her toes as she kicked her legs back and forth. "The first time was the worst," she said.

He hadn't quite figured out the conversation, but it sounded like she needed someone to listen to her, so he listened.

"I was upside down in the dunker when I had some sort of weird flashback." She stopped watching her toes and turned to him. "I think my dad drowned. My dad was a Navy SEAL and he drowned. Don't you find it ironic?" She laughed, but there was no humor in it.

"What makes you think he drowned?" he asked.

"I don't know." She shook her head. "Something I overheard at the funeral. I was mad at the world, and mad at him because no one remembered it was my birthday. I took Sam and crawled under a table in the corner to sing 'Happy Birthday' to myself. I remember a conversation between two men, one was very upset. He described a helicopter going down over water—the Mekong Delta. That's how I know it wasn't a training accident.

"My father wasn't the only man who died that day. His whole squad wound up dead. Mike," she hesitated, "I hit the water in that dunker and heard the pilot's voice retelling that tale as clearly as if it were yesterday. I didn't put it all together until a few days ago, but I think that pilot, the man talking, was Captain Loring."

Mike took her hand in his. Her fingers felt chilled, and he rubbed warmth into them. "Come here," he said, and pulled her into his arms.

She buried her face in his shoulder, and he held her tight. "Nobody wants me to do this," she said. "Nobody believes I can do this. Nobody understands why I have to. It's as if I have to go get him. Every pickup has to be perfect. If I do my job, nobody dies. Please, don't die, Mike."

"I can't make you any promises about tomorrow, but I have no intention of dying today," he said as he kissed away her tears. "Do you trust me?"

CHAPTER TEN

ACTIVITY FOR THE DAY. 0430 FRIDAY. ALTERNATE 10 MILE HIKE WITH PACK AND MONSTER MASH. ALL PERSONNEL. UNIFORM: BATTLE DRESS UNIFORM/ FULL PACK. REQ SOPA ADMIN PASS TO HCS-9 ANDST-11.

As soon as his feet hit the sand, Mike released the carabiner attached to his safety line. In one swift move he was free of the hovering Seahawk.

His "first into danger, last out" philosophy had earned him the respect of his entire team. They weren't exactly storming Tangos here in the Nevada desert, but that didn't mean he expected anything less than one hundred percent from his team.

He scrambled for the dune in the distance as if they were entering enemy territory and not running this scenario for the tenth time that morning. Most folks weren't even out of bed yet. "Hoo-yah!"

The downdraft from the rotor blades kicked up a cloud of dust as the helicopter hovered long enough to drop his four-man fire team. He covered his mouth and nose with a bandanna to keep from breathing in the sand.

If possible, it was going to be even hotter today than yesterday. He cleared the dune in an adrenaline-fueled rush and slid down the other side, heart racing. Itch, Ajax and Kip Nouri were right behind him. Weapon at the ready, Mike pulled down the bandanna and rolled to his belly. Taking a defensive posture, he fired off rounds of cover—live rounds—as his men joined in the firefight against an invisible foe.

A training op wasn't all that different from a real world op. Both were physically and mentally demanding. He thrived on the challenge. Lived on the edge. He hoped he'd die in his bed at the ripe old age of ninety-eight like his paternal grandfather, but if it was his time to go he wouldn't regret it. For one thing he wouldn't be leaving a wife and kids behind to grieve, the way Hannah still grieved for her father.

She needed closure.

He wished he could offer it.

"Cease fire," he ordered some time later, when the last member of his team had reached the dune. "Chief," he called to Itch. "Get on the horn. I think we can call it a day."

Itch radioed the Seahawks. "Thanks for the lift, Wings. We're gonna hoof it from here. Warriors need the exercise. Over and out."

"Copy BravoEleven," Calypso said. "NightHawk, Romeo five five, over and out."

"Gotta love a woman who knows how to handle a stick." The ever-pragmatic Itch said as the helicopters flew out of sight.

DOUGLAS HOUSE BACHELOR OFFICERS' QUARTERS
Fallon, Nevada

"Door's open." Hannah fanned herself in front of the open freezer in an attempt to stay cool. She couldn't imagine what McCaffrey's fire team was going through right now in this hundred-degree heat.

"AC out again?" Spence asked as he carried in bags from the Navy Exchange. "Whole building?"

"Afraid so."

"Something sweet and something salty." He stopped on the other side of the kitchen bar. Setting the bags on the counter, he pulled up a stool. "Change is in the bag."

Comfort food.

"Thanks." She opened the bag of chips and left them on the counter. Ben & Jerry's went in the freezer though she was tempted to smear it all over her body.

She blamed her cravings on the heat. And cramps. And all that endurance exercise. She must be burning at least an extra five hundred calories a day. Not to mention those she burned at night.

Except last night after she and McCaffrey had made love, and there was no more denying on her part that that's what it was, she'd realized she had to end it.

Spence grabbed a handful of chips and studied her as he munched. "You're sleeping with him," he said.

"Not anymore," she said, without denying what had been.

"So what happened last night to end it?"

"Other than he bound my hands and feet, threw me into the pool, then had his way with me? Nothing." She reached into the bag of potato chips

"Drown-proofing, right? Crazy guys tie each other up, bounce off the bottom of the pool and call themselves Navy SEALs…drown-proofing."

She stuffed her mouth and shrugged. Purposely leaving the situation open to his interpretation. Somewhere between drown-proofing and bondage came the most sensual experience of her life. *Do you trust me?*

"Feel like heading over to the Wing Nut for happy hour and a little karaoke?" Spence asked.

"It's always happy hour at the Wing Nut. Normally, I'd say no, but right now I'd agree to anything to get out of this heat. Even listening to some really bad music."

"It's not so bad. Maybe I'll even get you up on stage."

"Not on your life."

"We'll see. Webb and Boomer are coming. Let me grab a cold shower and I'll meet you back here in a half hour."

"Sounds good."

Spence picked up his bags and turned to leave. "Almost forgot—" he reached into one and pulled out a tiny white T-shirt "—I saw this and thought of you." He held up a shirt with the Oreo Cookie and Got Milk logos.

"How very commercial of you. And sweet. Thank you."

"If you don't think it fits, you can give it to Fallon," he teased, leaving it on the counter. Hannah made a quick call home before she stepped into the shower.

THE WING NUT
Fallon, Nevada

KARAOKE NIGHT at the Wing Nut brought the Naval Aviators out in force. Hannah took center stage after some serious coaxing from her co-pilot.

While Spence picked out sheet music for their duet, she twisted her watch again, not bothering to check the face since it would only be five minutes from the last time she'd looked.

"Testing, one, two." She cringed at the sound of her own voice.

Smiling in his easy manner, Spence made some final adjustments. "Eye on the screen. Wait for the color to change," he instructed her. After handing her a mike, he took the other for himself. "Don't worry. I'll cue you."

How had she ever let him talk her into this?

She managed a few deep breaths before the music started. Then stumbled over her first line when McCaffrey walked in the door. Mistaking her hesitation, Spence cued the music back to the beginning.

Hannah fixed her eyes on Mac. He stopped just inside the entrance. Arms crossed, he stared back at her while his men filed in around him.

After the initial eye contact, he sauntered over to

a table in the back, looking none the worse for his ten-mile hike out of the desert. Except for the sunburn.

Hannah tried to concentrate on the words that flashed on the screen. Spence's husky tenor had her singing along, which earned her appreciative whistles from the F-14 Tomcat pilots gathered up front.

But the words to "Cruisin'" were for Mac.

Mike leaned forward in his seat. He didn't like seeing Hannah standing up there with Spencer Holden. Mike had always thought the kid just wanted to do his duty. That is until Mike saw Holden hamming it up on stage with Hannah. Then it seemed as if the former teen idol wanted to do Hannah. And if those fly boys to his right didn't shut the hell up, they were going to be eating their teeth.

Last night he'd tied her ankles and wrists, binding her to him. Mind, body and soul.

Her heart still played hard to get.

And his was playing chicken.

The song ended. Mike didn't join in the applause. He kept his gaze locked with Hannah's as if he could pull her to him by sheer force of will.

It worked. She headed straight for him. Hannah was hot tonight, and it had nothing to do with the desert heat, and everything to do with the way she looked at him.

"A little aloe vera will take the sting out." She settled in at his table and took a sip of his beer.

"I've been stung worse. Care to explain the note you left me on your kitchen counter?"

"Can we take this outside?" she asked, sliding his beer toward him.

He got up without another word. Taking his beer, he steered her toward the nearest emergency exit, which had been propped open, working the AC over time. No alarms sounded when they left the bar, except for those going off in his head.

He'd known something was wrong last night when he'd brought her back to her room and she'd said good-night at the door. But he'd accepted sleeping alone as part of their bargain.

Cool professionals by day. Feverish lovers by night.

It made their lights-out sessions all the more exciting.

But last night he'd gone too far. He'd scared her. Not with the things he'd done, but with the things he'd made her feel. Hannah didn't like giving up control. He suspected this was her way of trying to get it back.

Gravel crunched beneath their boots as they headed to his Jeep, parked under a broken streetlight. Without saying a word, she put her purse on his hood and dug through it. She offered him some Chap Stick for his sun-blistered lips.

He shook his head and took a swig of beer instead. Planting his backside against the Jeep, he rested a booted foot on the bumper. "So you don't want to see me tonight, or ever again?" he said in reference to her note.

"That's not what I wrote."

"You have the floor." He toasted her with the beer.

"It's that time of the month. I tried to explain—"

"That you didn't want *sex* tonight. And since we're leaving here Sunday I no longer serve a useful purpose."

"To put it bluntly, yes. There's the picnic tomorrow with both our commands. Then we're back in Coronado."

"And you don't want to be seen at the picnic or in Coronado together because…" He gave her an opening, but she didn't fill in the blank, so he did. "For a woman it's a bad career move to be seen as open to dating a fellow officer? I'm really just guessing here, help me out."

"Close enough."

"FYI, Han, I haven't been coming around for the sex. It's been good, but not great—"

"Not great! You can say that after last night?"

In his mind's eye, shadow and light shimmered across the surface of the pool, bedeviling him with the memory of her wet and willing surrender.

"Great would be if we weren't hiding behind doors and in the dark. Last night was amazing, and I think that scared you. In case you haven't noticed, for some time now I haven't been running anywhere but toward you."

He could see the indecision in her eyes, in the way she bit down on her bottom lip. "Have you ever asked yourself why we only get together in Nevada, Mike? It's our fantasy world. It's not the real world of a Navy SEAL or a SpecWar pilot. It's not the civilian world in which I live or the Navy world in which you move. When we go home, things are different."

"We'll always have Fallon," he paraphrased the line from Casablanca. "Is that it? Then Fallon it is, get in," he said, dumping the rest of his beer to the dirt and throwing the bottle in back.

"What'd you have in mind?" She climbed in.

"Midnight picnic in the desert." He spun his tires as he left the parking lot. He was a man of action. And he'd already decided where all this was leading. He'd known it a year ago. Why fight it. "I'd like to keep driving straight through to Reno," he said when they hit the highway.

"And do what?"

"The grown-up thing. Get married. Whatever it takes to prove to you that I'm going to stick." He shifted his gaze from the road to her. "You're laughing."

"You're joking."

"Nobody would miss us until Monday."

"Are you suggesting we go AWOL to get married?"

"I'm suggesting we cut through all the crap and find a way to make it work. You, me and the Navy."

GRIME'S POINT
Fallon, Nevada

DINNER WAS A BUCKET of KFC. He'd driven out to Grime's Point, a prime stargazing or strategizing spot, depending on the intentions of the parties involved.

With a four-wheel drive they could get to a vantage point on the back side of the hills, away from the glare of the Naval base lights. They sat on the hood and leaned back against the windshield, gazing up at an inky sky counting stars. "Cold?" he asked, now that the sun had gone down.

"Not really," Hannah answered.

He took off his jacket anyway and draped it around her shoulders.

"That was rather chivalrous of you."

"Well, I did take the last drumstick, and I know dark meat is your favorite," he said, holding it up.

She picked at the white meat of the breast in her hand. "This is the only place on earth I can breathe. Endless desert. Endless sky. But you knew that, didn't you?"

"Why do you think I brought you here?"

In years past, they'd come here and shared a six-pack, then spent the night under the stars as friends. But a blanket of stars wasn't going to change her mind.

"I know there's something you're holding back, Han. I thought maybe we could talk about what's on your mind."

Most of the time it was Fallon on her mind. Or McCaffrey. Or Fallon and McCaffrey. "Yeah, there is," she admitted.

She put the half-eaten chicken breast back in the bucket and wiped her fingers on a moist towelette. Settling back against the windshield, she picked up her first long-neck of the night.

"Care to elaborate?" he asked.

"Don't you ever get stressed about anything?"

"When nobody's shooting at me, I figure I don't have too much to worry about."

"And when somebody *is* shooting at you?"

"I'm too busy to be worried."

"Well, I feel this terrible sense of foreboding, like something bad's going to happen." She dropped her head to her raised knees, resting it there briefly before turning to study his outline. "I worry about you."

He reached over with one hand and massaged the tension from the back of her neck. "I'm a big boy, Han. I can take care of myself."

His hand came to rest on the middle of her back. She could feel its warmth through the jacket he'd draped over her shoulders. "Do you ever think about what you'll do when you get out?"

He removed his hand. "Is this where you tell me you'll marry me if I consider a new line of work?"

"I'm not into ultimatums."

He fixed his gaze on the bottle in his hand. "But you'd like me to change…."

"I'd be a fool to think I could change you. An even bigger one to want to. I've never understood women who fall in love with a man and then want to change who he is—kind of makes you wonder if they've fallen in love with the man or the idea of falling in love."

He looked up from the bottle.

"And no, I still won't run away with you to Reno." She smiled sadly into the darkness.

"There's middle ground in there somewhere, Han."

"I don't see it."

"Maybe you're just not looking hard enough. If two people want to make it work they find a way."

"Not always. I don't think we can. For the same reasons you won't give up your command for a woman, I can't give up mine for a man."

"What's there to give up? You're active duty for twenty-four months, then you're back to being a weekend warrior. Your current situation is temporary at best."

"That's the problem. But let's say it isn't. You're the last man who can give me guarantees, but say two years from now I'm a civilian sailor again and you're still going strong as a Navy SEAL. I live in Colorado. I want kids."

She didn't need light to see the stubborn set to his jaw. "Kids." He shook his head. "That's the real fork in the road, isn't it?"

"Why? Why not kids? The world's a big bad place and you don't want to bring children into it?" That had been her own excuse once.

"You know I don't believe that."

"Then why?"

"It's hard to explain."

"Try."

"It's complicated. Kids are a big responsibility. I like not having that responsibility. Not everyone wants kids."

"Time and circumstance aren't small divides that

can be crossed easily. When one partner wants children and the other doesn't, that's a pretty big divide."

"Because I don't want children? I recall a conversation in which you didn't want children. You had a career to think about and—"

"And I thought the world was a big bad place. I don't anymore." She felt the vibration of her pager. "I need you to want children, Mike."

"It's not going to happen." He checked his own pager. "I have to take this call."

"Me, too." There was a plague in her perfect place. She wanted to tell him about his daughter. And now she knew she never would.

CHAPTER ELEVEN

NAVAL AMPHIBIOUS BASE
Coronado, California

"THE PHILIPPINE GOVERNMENT has a longstanding ban on foreign troops participating in combat on their soil." Admiral Bell began their briefing while his aide passed out folders. Hannah accepted hers with a polite, out-of-place "thank you," which echoed through the war room. McCaffrey glanced at her with a frown before setting his stern concentration back on the admiral.

"Three years ago Abu Sayyaf guerrillas set up camp on Basilan Island in order to conduct their campaign of mass kidnappings and killings throughout the Philippines. Foreign investments and tourism suffered. In counterterrorism maneuvers last year, U.S. Special Forces—in an advisory role to the Filipino Army—helped wipe out the guerrillas there. But the six months of training exercises sparked controversy.

"As you know, the P.I. gained its independence from the U.S. on July 4, 1946, and they're eager to maintain it. Their president has made very public statements denying U.S. participation in this fight against Muslim extremists. We are not to do anything that will embarrass our former colony. I hope I'm making myself clear?"

The admiral's question, of course, was rhetorical.

"SEALs acted as forward observers last year, conducting an intel sweep of the islands to the south of Basilan. You'll note in Commander McCaffrey's report…"

Hannah flipped open her folder and scanned the top page. She stole a look at McCaffrey. He hadn't just written the report, he'd led the recon.

"Is everyone on the same page?" the admiral asked before continuing. "The network of islands in this region, many with structures built by the Japanese and the Americans in World War II, make it almost impossible to locate every last participant." Admiral Bell drew their attention to the enlarged map on the wall behind him.

"But Mac anticipated the remaining members of Abu Sayyaf would regroup on Jolo and identified Muslim separatists that might sympathize with the guerrillas. One of those splinter groups, al-Ayman, already has a stronghold on that island."

He paused for a moment to let his words sink in.

"As predicted, the two groups have joined forces. Original estimates on the number of guerrillas thought to have escaped Basilan have more than doubled. And al-Ayman has ten times that number. The Philippine army is going to be confronting a small army of terrorists while America and the rest of the free world is otherwise occupied in the Gulf."

Hannah tensed. If she felt this shell-shocked after receiving her first real-world mission, how was she going to fare when bullets started flying?

Real bullets.

Her men were counting on her. McCaffrey and his men were counting on her and their daughter was counting on her.

No more "pleases" and "thank-yous." She'd come to play with the big boys and she had to act like one. "What do we know about al-Ayman, Admiral?"

"The Holy Right Hand, the hand of judgment, as they like to call themselves was started by this man." An out-of-focus picture came on the screen. "Mullah Kahn, the Cobra. One of the top-ten terrorists in the world, and we don't even have a decent picture of this guy. Just last year we caught and locked up two of his sons. It's been personal ever since.

"Calypso, HCS-9 will be flying support for the SEALs and any additional duties assigned to your squadron by the military liaison at base camp X-Ray. Mac, Team Eleven will be island-hopping to the south and west of Jolo, serving as forward observers."

"Is anyone actually going to use the intel this time?" McCaffrey asked.

"That's not your concern. Gather intelligence. That's it."

"And if we get shot at?"

"Your mission is recon only. Do not engage the enemy."

"And if the enemy engages us?"

"The official U.S. position is that you'll need permission from your Filipino counterparts before engaging in any combat. These are the rules of your engagement. Gentlemen, kiss your sweethearts goodbye. We've got a job to do."

HANNAH RETURNED home to pack clean underwear and squeeze in some precious minutes with her daughter. The movers had come, but Hannah's bedroom looked and felt more like storage than living space.

"How long will you be gone?" Sammy asked, trying to make herself useful by gathering Hannah's dirty laundry.

"I don't know." Hannah held Fallon while she lifted folded underwear out of her drawer and transferred it to her seabag. Two weeks without her daughter had been too much. Fallon had grown so big Hannah couldn't imagine leaving her for two months. Or more.

She kissed her baby's downy head and let Sammy finish her packing.

"Well, where are you going?" her mother asked as she stepped into the room.

"You know I can't tell you that," Hannah said, padlocking her seabag. Amazing what she could do with one hand when she had to.

She didn't want to put Fallon down, but she gave her to Sammy. The baby started to cry, which had Hannah starting. "Mommy will be back as soon as she can, sweetheart. I promise."

BASILAN ISLAND
Philippine Islands

ONE MONTH, several phone calls home and several islands later, Hannah found herself looking forward to
the few minutes McCaffrey would spend in her Seahawk. Each time she picked him up he looked a little grungier, and each time she dropped him off she
hit "Cruisin'" on the CD player.

The man might be in his element, but she couldn't
help but feel apprehensive leaving him until the next
time she saw him.

She'd medevaced several wounded Philippine soldiers by this time and had even extracted some under
fire. One of McCaffrey's men had suffered a nasty
fall, and she'd gone in after him, as well. He was now
laid up with a sprained ankle. A quick check on his
injured man had been McCaffrey's only trip back to
base camp X-Ray in a month.

Today her gunship crews were headed out earlier
than usual now that their pickup points were getting
farther out.

She'd gathered her pilots and crews in the Quon-
set hut that served as their ready room. "Time hack,"
she called. "For 2030 hours." Her pilots fiddled with
the setting on their watches as she counted down on
hers. "Five, four, three, two, one…*hack.*"

Married men twisted off wedding rings and
stowed them in their lockers so they wouldn't catch
them and lose a finger. The first items on their list

completed, she called attention to the navigation logs, maps and weather charts spread out on the table and briefed the men on their mission.

Coordinates had to be figured with precision. One degree off course could put them a mile off target— a mere pencil line on a map, but unacceptable in a covert pickup.

Being good with sticks and switches wasn't good enough for a Special Warfare pilot. A conventional helicopter pilot could err on the side of safety, a Seahawk pilot had to be on target every time—no matter what the hazard.

At 2030 hours they set their watches. At 2245 hours they were strapped into the cockpit. At 2255 hours they started their engines and ran through preflight checks.

The rumble from the eight gunships on the tarmac reached a deafening roar. Earplugs filtered out the worst of the background noise while earphones crackled with crew chatter. On top of that Hannah had a dozen radio frequencies to monitor.

"Number one engine? Started," she asked, and answered herself, continuing down the laminated engine-start checklist on her knee. Nothing was left to chance. "Throttle. Set. Fuel-control levers. Open."

Rotor blades turned at exactly 2300 hours.

She ran through her before-taxiing checklist. Ground crews pulled the blocks from under the wheels, and she moved her gunship down the taxiway.

Keeping cyclic stick and pedals steady, she pulled

back on the collective, lifting her Seahawk off the ground. The helo shook, rattled and rolled out.

"Goggles up," Hannah ordered, dropping her own night-vision goggles into place and her world turned monochromatic green.

She hit play on the CD player and "Playing With the Boys" came on. They were flying in pairs with Parish's gunship trailing hers.

About ten klicks out from their pickup a broken call came through on the frequency they used to monitor the SEALs.

"Medevac."

"Did you copy that, Spence?"

"Sounded like a call for a medevac."

"That's what I heard. Can you repeat?" she asked in the mike.

The next stream of communication came through in local dialect.

"Anyone speak Tagalog?" Hannah asked, knowing that her crew didn't, but recognizing enough of the language to realize that's what it was.

"Can you repeat in English?" she asked the distressed caller.

"—injured man—requesting medevac to Basilan Island…"

"Please identify yourself."

The soldier complied as requested and even knew the proper codes and passwords.

"That was yesterday's password," Webb, their most experienced crew member, pointed out.

Hannah checked her watch. "Copy that, Chief."

"Maybe he didn't get the updates yet," Spence said. "How many times were we late getting ours?"

"Your location?" Hannah asked so she could determine, which two gunships might be close enough to break away for an emergency medical evacuation.

He gave them coordinates to the island where they were to extract Team Eleven's Bravo Squad. Several miles separated the two points, but if she adjusted her speed by a few knots she could make the evac and still be on time to pick up Mac.

"Hollywood, get BravoEleven on line. We'll proceed with caution," she said to the crew. To the distressed caller, she said, "This is NightHawk, Romeo five five," giving their squadron call sign and her gunship number. "We're on our way."

HANNAH FILLED IN Parish en route, and he maintained his course behind Hannah. When they reached the island, radar gave her an image of what was going on outside her Seahawk.

"There," Spence said, picking up the bright green spot not far from the beach at the north end of the island.

She flew in closer. No hot spots or unusual activity in the jungle to indicate an ambush. Their evac appeared to be what he said he was—a lone man. But Hannah couldn't shake her bad feeling. "Something's not right," she said, sharing her suspicions with her crew.

"I agree," Webb said.

Rotor wash whipped back up from the ground as she hovered over their target. Hannah stabilized the control stick near her left knee, mindful that inaction made them sitting ducks. "I'm going in," she informed both crews. "Boomer, keep that machine gun pointed right at him. Fifty mm of threat should keep him from doing anything stupid. Chief, you nab and grab." She then broadcast instructions to the injured soldier, "Hands on your head. Then on your knees."

He complied.

She touched down. The Crew Chief hopped out, pulled the man to his feet and assisted him, none too gently, into the back of the helo while patting him down for any undisclosed weapons. "He's clean."

Up close the man wore the uniform of the Philippine army. His battered face and torso, visible because of his open shirt, suggested a severe beating. Webb gave him the courtesy helmet so Hannah could speak to him, and he introduced himself once again, "Sergeant Wray…Philippine Special Forces."

"Our pleasure, Wray," Hannah said as she took the bird up. "Have you reached McCaffrey yet?" she asked Spence.

"The Americans?" Wray asked. "When my teammate and I were captured yesterday. We saw Americans. They're being held by al-Ayman to the southwest. I escaped. My teammate was not as fortunate—they beat him to death."

"Maybe the SEALs escaped." The statement was a prayer.

"No," Wray said.

"What do you do for the army, Wray?" Webb asked.

"Scout. I'm a scout. Special Forces. Recon."

"How many Americans?"

Hannah could tell by Webb's questions that he wasn't going to trust Wray.

If a scout could escape, A SEAL could escape. And eight SEALs could turn a terrorist camp upside down.

Flying parallel to the island, toward her southwest target, she reached the extraction point a few minutes later. But Mac's fire team wasn't there, and they still hadn't broken radio silence. She waited fifteen minutes past their rendezvous time before making the decision to leave. If there was a Tango camp on the island, a visual would help, at least it would be something she could take back to the rest of McCaffrey's SEAL Team along with Sergeant Wray.

Like her crew chief, she wasn't ready to take their passenger at his word. But she did know one thing— with a member of the Philippine army on board she could shoot real bullets.

"You don't mind if we take you on a little training op, do you, Sarg?" Without waiting for his answer, she pointed the joystick to the southwest, not too far from the extraction location.

Flashes of light appeared in the jungle. Gunfire.

"Romeo five five." Someone from the ground

hailed their gunship. They could clearly hear the gunfire from his mike.

"It's McCaffrey," Spence said.

"Copy, BravoEleven. Hang on, we're coming to get you out."

"Negative. Negative. Do not attempt extract—at this time…." His com was breaking up. *"Under heavy fire—enemy engaged…"*

That didn't make any sense. If he and his men were under fire they'd want to be pulled out. Their mission was recon. They'd be severely outnumbered and unable to engage the enemy. Other voices came through the line in a mix of Tagalog and English, but clearly calling for her help.

"BravoEleven, we're coming in with air cover."

"Negative. Abort."

He wanted her to abort? Leave him and his men there to face the enemy alone? Because of her? She could see them now. The SEALs, identifiable by the glow-in-the-dark markings on their left shoulders, running with fire power on their heels. Where were they running to if not to her?

"It's your call," Parish advised over the radio, in a rather transparent attempt to make the decision for her.

"Eyes open. We're going in—danger close!" she ordered, swooping in with a slashing L attack. With friendlies in the line of fire, they were extra cautious. The second gunship fell in right behind her.

Boomer fired a hail of bullets stopping the line of

advance and giving the SEALs more time to distance themselves from the enemy. The ping of responding fire meant they were now the prime targets. If she turned, she'd be exposing her vulnerable starboard side, but then she'd be closing off the enemy's line of attack and that's what she wanted them to do.

She made a quick right while the trailer ship was still engaged, then came back around while Parish turned. They managed to keep the enemy pinned down this way for several minutes.

"Stinger!" Spence warned a split second before the warning went off in the cockpit. Parish's Seahawk exploded in a ball of fire.

"Seahawk down," Webb shouted.

Oh, God. Hannah breathed a silent prayer. "Where'd these guys get RPGs!" She banked the gunship to dodge a hail of bullets while trying to confuse the rocket-propelled grenades with chafe and flares. Metallic pings told her she hadn't avoided all fire. "Status report," she called to her crew. They were losing altitude. Fast. She fought the collective to keep the helicopter under control.

"We've been hit. Tail rotor," Webb shouted.

"Mainframe tank," Spence echoed, shutting off the fuel transfer from the wing tanks and switching to their remaining main tank. They needed more than the six hands, Hannah, her co-pilot and her crew chief had to operate the switches and toggles and sticks. Their gunner was busy with a fire in back and Wray was just in the way.

"TF fail." She watched the monitors go black as they continued spiraling out of control. Hannah glanced over at the picture of her daughter tucked next to the screen. Her every correction had to be perfect, or it would be her last.

"Buckle in!" she ordered the crew.

"Stinger," Spence warned.

Too late. They plummeted toward the ground.

CHAPTER TWELVE

MIKE RACED to the downed helos with one thought—to reach Hannah before al-Ayman did. He could smell the fuel even before he could see it.

Webb Emerson staggered from the wreckage, hauling Boomer out by the scruff. Boomer pushed to stand on his uninjured leg, and Webb assisted the gunner to the tree line before heading back with Mike after the pilot and co-pilot.

Spence had launched headfirst into the now-shattered Plexiglas windshield and hung half in, half out of the gunship. The man groaned as Webb eased his body through the opening. The mike had torn through his nose and mouth, leaving his face bloody and unrecognizable.

Mike crawled over him to reach Hannah, her limp body still strapped to the seat. He left her helmet on, as per standard operating procedure.

"Hannah," he called to her, desperate for a response. He found a thready pulse at the base of her throat. She was still alive.

But she didn't make a sound as he freed her from

the seat, threw her over his shoulder in a fireman carry and scrambled out of the burning helo.

"We've got to move now," Itch shouted.

"There's one more," Webb called to them. "An evac—"

Itch raced for the helo even as a series of small explosions started erupting around the wreckage.

"No!" Mike shouted, setting Hannah down to follow Itch at a dead run. He was not going to send another man home in a body bag just because his chief was hell-bent on being some sort of damn superhero.

Mike slammed Itch to the ground. The fuel tank exploded in one big fireball.

He ducked for cover from the hot shrapnel raining down. "You okay?" He choked back the black billowing smoke.

"Yeah. You?"

Mike checked the rip in his sleeve, just a graze. "Yeah." A few more inches and the razor-sharp metal would have come close to taking his arm off. He pushed to his feet but didn't bother dusting off. The game was just getting started.

He picked up Hannah again and carried her while Webb and Hazard supported Boomer in a five-legged race. Four of Mike's men carried Holden, each holding a corner of the makeshift stretcher, a thermal blanket generally used for shock.

Itch guarded their exposed tails as they attempted to lose the guerrillas in the thick brush and darkness. The plants slapped at them and slowed their progress, but they didn't have time to break out the machetes, nor did they want to leave a trail.

Nouri had been sent for a sitRep of the other gunship and crew, and he finally caught up to them. "The good news is all four of them walked away from the crash. The bad news is al-Ayman got there first."

"Any sign that we're being followed?"

"Al-Ayman is too busy celebrating their capture to care much about us. They're headed back to camp. Not so much as a scout on our tail."

"Itch," Mike called out. "Let's slow it down and pay a little more attention to covering our trail. Give it a klick or two, and we'll stop to check on our wounded."

His muscles strained from the extra weight, but he'd carry Hannah all night if he had to. Still unsure of the extent of her injuries, he wanted to give her as smooth a ride as possible. He prayed there was no internal damage done.

Why the hell hadn't she aborted when he'd ordered her to? They'd discovered the stingers, but in the process had been discovered themselves. Ground-to-air weapons made this group much more dangerous to the gunships than to his team.

After another klick and further confirmation that they weren't being followed, Mike called a halt and lowered Hannah to the ground.

Boomer barely made a whimper in spite of his obvious discomfort, which was a good thing since it wasn't life threatening. He had to wait until the corpsman could assess the damage to Hannah and Holden.

"Holden's lost a lot of blood." Hospital Corpsman Ryan "Doc" Brady reported. "He's in shock. Otherwise in good shape, except for his face."

"What's his blood type? Does he need a field transfusion?"

"I don't think so. Not yet anyway. I can keep him hydrated and the pain at bay with morphine. But if we're going to be here for any length of time I'm going to have to stitch him up. You know how easy it is for infection to set in out here. I've got the antibiotics, but they won't do much good for a gaping wound."

"So stitch him up."

"Mac, it's Hollywood. His face…" Doc kept his voice to a whisper. "This guy needs a reconstructive surgeon. I'm just a field medic."

"He can have reconstructive surgery after you save his life."

"He won't let me touch him until I've seen to Calypso. How is she?"

"Unconscious." The weight of that one word felt heavy in his chest.

"Head injury, you think?" Doc knelt beside Mike so he could take a closer look. "She's still wearing her crash helmet. That's good." Brady handed him smelling salts.

"Hannah," Mike called her name as he held the salts under her nose.

She stirred, groaned. Her eyes blinked open.

She stared up at him with a dazed look on her face. "How many fingers am I holding up?"

She sprang to a sitting position and pushed his hand aside. "Parish's gunship. Spence is hurt—" She didn't wait for help to get up. She assessed the gathered group, removed her helmet and crawled toward Holden.

Mike tried to warn her. "Han—"

"Spence," she said, taking his hand.

He opened his eyes. "Hannah," he managed to say.

"I'm right here," she said, brushing the blood-matted hair back from his forehead.

As Doc moved to clean him up, Holden batted at his hand.

"You're going to have to let him sew you up, Spence."

"My face—" He turned to spit blood, but coughed instead.

"Hollywood," she said. "Trust me. Chicks dig guys with scars. Think of all that time you're going to get to spend with your Navy nurse."

"I love you, Hannah." He lifted his hand to brush her cheek with his knuckles. She squeezed his hand. "I didn't want to leave anything unsaid."

"I love you, too." She choked back a sob. "Hang in there, okay. Let Doc sew you up."

"Don't leave anything left unsaid."

"Okay," she promised as he closed his eyes to the jab of Doc's needle. Instead of leaving his side, Hannah stayed until Doc finished the job.

When she pushed to her feet, she almost collapsed against Mike. He steadied her. "Don't read too much into that little love scene. All guys love their swim buddies after some morphine." He knew the *I love yous* came before the morphine, but maybe she didn't.

Hannah held on to him as she reached for the nearest tree. Then she let go and threw up on his boots. She wiped her mouth on her sleeve. "Where's Wray?"

"Wray who?" He wiped his boots on the underbrush.

"Our pickup," she said, swaying on her feet.

"Dead," he said without mincing words. He handed her his canteen.

She took a swallow and spit. "And Parish?"

"Alive."

He saw the hope in her eyes.

"Captured," he said. "Whole crew."

"We're going after them."

"*We* doesn't include *you*."

She staggered back a few steps, drew her handgun and fired.

"What the—" Mike was still patting his chest in amazement, looking for bullet holes long after he realized she'd fired over his shoulder.

"I wasn't aiming for you, McCaffrey. If I had been I would have aimed lower," she said before she fainted.

MIKE BARELY HAD TIME to catch her before she hit the ground. He settled her there then raised his weapon.

Kip and Itch already had their weapons pointed. Itch ventured farther into the jungle, then lowered his rifle.

Mike came up beside him. A Filipino with two holes in his head lay lifeless.

"He's dead," Itch said.

Mike checked—no pulse. Two holes—no kidding.

"Wray," he read the name sewn to the man's uniform and let out an uneasy breath.

"She was obviously delirious," Itch said. "His weapon was drawn. She saw movement, an honest mistake."

But a mistake just the same. There'd be hell to pay for killing an allied soldier. In a training accident no less.

"Did you see him draw his weapon?" Mike asked Itch.

Itch shook his head. "But come on…he's armed—"

Mike unholstered his handgun and, without hesitation, shot off two rounds into the nearest tree trunk. He looked both Itch and Kip in the eye. "She didn't kill him. I did."

Both men offered a solemn nod, as good as their word. They might not like it, but they'd back up his story.

Mike digitally recorded the man from the shoulders up. The evidence he'd take back would show two bullets to the head. By the time the body was recovered, if at all, no one would bother to dispute his story.

He took one of Sergeant Wray's dog tags and pocketed it. "Bury him in a shallow gave. Mark the location for recovery. But try to conceal it from al-Ayman," he instructed without ceremony.

Hannah sat a few yards away, her face covered by her hands. He tugged them free. "Move out," he ordered. He had to get her moving before shock took over, if it hadn't already.

"I killed a man," she sobbed. "I looked him in the eye, just like you said not to, and I killed him."

"You missed him by a mile. I killed him."

She stared at him with a blank look on her face. "I—"

"I did," he insisted.

"Why would you say something like that?"

He looked her in the eyes. "Because it's the truth."

WHAT DID MCCAFFREY THINK he was protecting her from? The truth? She'd killed a man, an ally, and she had to live with that, even if it meant going to prison. Under the same circumstances, she'd do it again. When Wray had appeared out of the bushes and aimed that handgun at McCaffrey's back, countless regrets had flashed in her mind, not the least of which was that she'd never told Mike about their daughter.

The timing would never be perfect, so why not now?

Now, when his jaw held that foreboding line.

Now, when he pushed them through the jungle in the opposite direction of the guerrilla camp.

Now.

She had really lousy timing.

Hannah raced ahead to speak with Webb and Boomer. "Chief, Boomer, you both still have your handguns?" It was obvious when she approached that they both still wore their holsters with their sidearms in place. But they verbally confirmed it. "What about Spence?"

"Doc—" Webb used a headset given to him by the SEALs "—does Holden have his 9mm with him?"

"Negative."

Hannah heard the exchange as well as everyone else in their group.

"Did you catch that?" she asked McCaffrey.

He gripped her by the elbow and kept her moving. "Doesn't mean a thing."

"You think I killed an innocent man, but don't you see…that proves my case. He stole a weapon and disappeared, until he reappeared to take aim at your back—"

"Any trained soldier is going to reach for the nearest weapon. We didn't know he was there so we overlooked him in the confusion of pulling your crew from the wreckage. If he was trailing us, he could have shot me at any time. Instead he waited until we stopped and popped up to let us know that he was there. You're the only one who saw him take aim. And Hannah, you're in no condition—"

"He lied to us. He said Americans had been captured."

"Maybe we're not the only Americans on the island. Maybe al-Ayman captured Americans on another island and brought them here. We don't know he lied until we can check out the Tango's camp. And you're overlooking one very important fact—he's Filipino, not Arab. Al-Ayman is made up of Arab Muslim Extremists."

"What about his being a sympathizer? Or a brainwashed soldier? Or one of a dozen other explanations?"

"I'm open to the possibility. But it's my job to report the facts."

"I'm the one who shot and killed Sergeant Wray," she said.

"The facts are Wray was Filipino. He was wearing the uniform of the Philippine army. He came up on me from behind, weapon drawn. I turned and fired, putting two bullets in his head. And you are not the one going to Leavenworth for this." He said it with conviction. Who wouldn't believe him?

She grabbed his forearm and pulled him to a halt. "You can't protect me from something I did."

"Han, it's not up for debate."

She didn't doubt that he'd put his life on the line for her. She'd do the same for him. But a federal penitentiary? For a crime he didn't commit and she did? One of them had to watch his back.

And both of them had to be there to look after

their daughter. Spence was right. She shouldn't leave anything left unsaid.

She could have died today. She could still die today. And Mike could die. But the only real risk was that Fallon would never know her father.

That wasn't going to happen.

"Can we fall back. There's something—"

"Now is not the time or place for confessions. The touchy-feely crap is going to have to wait. I have two things on my mind. The first is keeping you safe, the second is rescuing your cr—"

"You have a daughter. *We* have a daughter."

CHAPTER THIRTEEN

MIKE HAD THREE THINGS on his mind now. The low blow Hannah had delivered did what the hike had been unable to do—knock the wind out of him. But he kept walking, picking his way through the dense undergrowth and rugged terrain of the jungle. This load was heavier than a hundred-and-thirty-pound woman, and all of it was in his head. Amazing what that extra burden could do to a man.

Hannah had given birth to *his* child and hadn't even bothered to tell him. It seemed shooting men in cold blood was something the woman excelled at.

Mike twisted the watch on his wrist. The Chase-Durer had no place here, but he'd finally decoded the message.

No regrets. Fallon.

What an idiot he'd been. He'd forever regret not taking a closer look at the little girl when he'd had the chance. He remembered her as pink. But what color were her eyes? Her hair? Did she look like him, even a little? Or did she look like Hannah?

"Say something," she said.

He kept walking. He had to keep walking until he distanced himself from feeling. He had a job to do.

"Mike—"

"That's Commander McCaffrey, or Mac to you. There is no Mike on this mission. Your timing could have been better, Stanton. Work on that!"

By the time they reached their staging area, a WWII bunker built into the side of a cliff by the Japanese, Mike had managed to tuck away his feelings into a neat little pigeonhole, just like the mail awaiting his return.

If they got out of this, he'd deal with everything Stateside.

Their command post had no door, except the vines that had grown over the opening. Mike upended his flashlight, giving the bunker a soft glow. Another gave off enough light to see by, but in the interest of conserving batteries they were only using the two. His SEALs had already spent three days on the island; supplies were running low.

"Set him over there." Doc had the stretcher bearers lay Holden on one of two tables in the room. While Doc tended to the wounded, Webb and Hannah joined his men in going over their hand-drawn maps of the island.

Mike couldn't even look at Hannah, so he addressed Webb. "Where did Wray say that guerrilla camp is supposed to be?"

"To the southwest," Hannah answered.

"That's the direction we were headed when we

stumbled on those stingers," Nouri said, setting aside his sniper rifle and easing out of his pack. Overeager and always the first to speak up, even when he shouldn't, Ensign Kip Nouri was the new guy. A blond beach bum and champion surfer, who'd made it through BUD/S, but still had six months of on-the-job training before he earned his budwiser.

"The guerrillas retreated in that direction," Itch added his own commentary to Nouri's.

The exact opposite end of the island, with only a few hours till sunup. Mike stood with his arms folded. "We can't afford to sit out the day in this bunker. The clock is ticking."

If the crew was in fact still alive, and he believed that was a strong possibility, considering the enemy's game plan. Four hostages would get them more attention than four dead men. But when the guerrillas were done with them, what then?

Mike shook his head over the maps. "We're just wasting time here. We need a visual on the layout of the camp. Number of guerrillas. Types of weapons. Modes of transportation, including to and from this island. There's that small settlement to the south, and the network of dirt roads running through there. It could be they're interacting, even living among the villagers."

Doc stepped over to their table. "Holden seems to be stable right now. But I should stay with him—"

"I'll take that under advisement," Mike said. "But we're going to need all the firepower and every able-bodied man we can spare." He sensed Hannah's growing unease from the opposite end of the table. "There's the possibility of other American and Filipino hostages aside from our four-man crew."

"*Every* able-bodied man?" Ajax nodded toward Hannah in an unspoken signal to Mike.

"I can still shoot." Boomer hobbled closer.

"I'm counting on that," Mike said. "You'll have to stand watch here. I don't want to draw too much attention by calling in another chopper until we've located Parish and the others. Doc, you'll stay with Spence. Keep him stable until we can get him the hell out of here." That left seven SEALs, including himself, to get the job done. Webb would be an additional asset. Hannah was his one liability. He knew she wasn't going to like his next order. He lifted his gaze to meet hers. "Stanton, extraction point Echo is just above this ridge. Give us until dawn and then call in the cavalry to get you out of here. If we've secured the prisoners, we'll be waiting for our ride at extraction point Sierra Whiskey. Webb, you'll be coming with us."

The men gathered their gear.

Worst case, they might need a lift out of Hotel Zulu—the hot zone.

"Move out," he ordered. Webb, Ajax, Itch, Nouri, Hazard, Sandman and Don Juan Costas exited the bunker—in that order, leaving Holden with Doc Brady, Boomer and Hannah. Doc had the only automatic weapon in the bunker, and Mike wanted to ensure there was a handgun for each of them. Keeping Holden's weapon, he checked his own 9mm Glock and chambered a round. He handed it to Hannah.

She let him get all the way out the bunker door before she said anything. "Commander."

He'd been hoping to avoid this.

His waiting men moved ahead of them. "You're staying," he said. She stuck like dog doody to the sole of his boot until he had no choice but to turn around and confront her.

"*Every* able-bodied man," she said. "We've rehearsed this exact scenario in training."

"Do I have to state the obvious?"

"You're changing the rules."

"The rules always excluded you, Stanton. We just let you play. SECNAVINST 1300.12B, paragraph 5a. Direct Ground Combat Rule. 'Service members are eligible to be assigned to all positions for which they are qualified, except that *women* shall be excluded from assignment to units whose primary mission is to engage in direct combat on the ground as defined…' Do you want me to *define* paragraph 5b?"

"You're forgetting the exception, Commander. 'Women Officer Aviators may be permanently assigned without restrictions to all aviation squadrons regardless of type mission,'" she quoted OPNAV-INST 1300.17, paragraph 3f. "That includes combat."

"I don't have time to debate Navy regs, so I'm just going to pull rank."

"Commander. It's my crash. My crew. My mess. I'm going to clean it up."

"Fine," he said.

Her momentary shock gave him time to act.

A quick knee to the back of hers and he dropped her to the ground. When she was facedown in the dirt, hands behind her back, he wedged his leg between her thighs.

"You want to go? You've got thirty seconds to get out of this hold."

"Get off me!" she demanded.

"Twenty-five. And I ain't even trying."

She struggled beneath his weight.

"Fifteen."

"I hate you!" She spit out dirt with her words.

"I don't care how you feel about me. This is not personal." Lifting her head by her hair, he bent to whisper in her ear. "This is the position you're going to find yourself in if you're captured. Am I making myself clear? Because unless you can prove to me you can fight your way out of it, I'm not letting you go, no matter what you say. So just cry uncle now!"

She went limp. He let go of her hair.

"Five, four, three, two and one." He sat back on his haunches. "You're staying. And that's an order, Commander, with all the weight of the Uniform Code of Military Justice behind it."

She rolled over and slapped him hard across the cheek. He didn't flinch.

"Ouch." Itch flinched for him. "Didn't see that

coming." He raised his voice with a fair amount of sarcasm. "Enough, Mac, let's go!"

"If you'd've hit me with a closed fist," Mike said to Hannah. "I might have reconsidered." He pushed to his feet. "You fight like a girl, Stanton. That's my point."

As it was, he had a hard time leaving her. The bunker was relatively safe. But the only place he could guarantee her safety was right behind him. He'd protect the mother of his child with his last breath if he had to.

HANNAH STEPPED outside the bunker. It was still dark, but the stars overhead were starting to vanish one by one. Boomer was standing watch and snubbed out his half-smoked cigarette, probably thinking she was going to give him a hard time about it, like she usually did.

"Got another one of those?" she asked.

Boomer patted down his pocket and tapped out a cigarette. Hannah put it to her lips, cupping her hands to protect it from the slight breeze as he lit it.

"How's Spence?" he asked, putting away his lighter.

He'd fallen back asleep after a period of unrest. "Quiet now," she said, exhaling the smoke.

"I didn't know you smoked."

"I have a lot of bad habits you don't know about, Boomer." She handed back the cigarette after that single drag. She didn't smoke, and he hadn't had anything more than Tylenol for the pain his leg must be causing him. Now was not the time and place to change her gunner's bad habits.

"Thanks," he said.

"I've got to answer nature's call," she said, moving away from the bunker.

"Should I go with you?" His normally deep voice cracked like a teenager's, and he cleared his throat. "Commander McCaffrey gave me explicit orders not to let you out of my sight—"

"I don't think he meant for you to watch me that close," she reassured him. For all she knew McCaffrey meant exactly that. He wasn't who she thought he was.

He'd challenged her authority and questioned her ability to do the job—all in front of the men. Sure, she could wallow in the aftermath of the crash, second-guess herself. But she'd made a judgment call when she'd flown in to save his ass, and she'd made a judgment call when she'd shot Wray. Men in her position did that all the time and weren't treated like second-class citizens for it.

Following the trail, Hannah fought the palm fronds that slapped her in the face. On top of everything else, McCaffrey hadn't asked one question about their daughter.

Her timing could have been better?

What about his timing?

She yanked down on the two-way zipper of her flight suit, yet another reason to feel inferior. She had to strip down just to pee.

Hannah was putting things back in place when she heard the first shot ring out.

FOUR HOURS LATER Mike was still rubbing the sting from his cheek. No time to stop and ease his bruised ego. They'd had to hoof it to reach the other side of the island in time for a predawn rescue.

The structure looked very much like a prisoner-of-war camp left over from WWII. The vines had grown up around the barbed wire, dragging it down. At least half of it was laid flat out. The rust would do more harm than the barbs that crumbled at a touch. Salt and sea air had done its damage.

"Ambush?" Itch asked from right beside him.

Mike flipped up his NVGs. It was too quiet down there.

Hannah had been positive Sergeant Wray was leading her crew into some kind of ambush. For everyone's sake he hoped the sergeant turned out to be one of the bad guys. Mike had his doubts about that. Still he had his men take every precaution as they moved through the dense undergrowth. They'd lost the element of surprise yesterday and could very well be walking into a trap today.

Still he was rather disappointed to discover the guerrillas' base camp didn't even boast so much as one alert sentry. The few men on guard duty strolled the grounds or chatted casually.

The one remaining dilapidated tower wasn't even in use.

In spite of its age, it was obvious the camp had been taken over as some sort of Tango training facility.

"I only have visual on a dozen Ts," Nouri whispered through his comm while setting up his high-powered rifle and scope. "There were at least twice that many when the helos went down."

"Maybe we're that lucky and they're that stupid," Ajax said in hushed tones.

"We're not that lucky." Mike trained his NVGs on a guarded barracks in the distance. "But it does look like they're that stupid. They're holding them all in one building—that should make our job easier." He laid out the plan, giving each man specific instructions.

"Mac," Nouri whispered into his mike.

Mike returned his attention to the camp.

The vine-covered main gates swung open. Three rusted Chevy trucks carrying at least a dozen men rolled into the center of camp, then stopped. The men started unloading, none too gently, a stretcher from the back of the second vehicle.

Mike took a deep breath and pushed his NVGs into place.

"They found them," Itch said. "They've got Holden. Boomer can barely stand on his broken leg, but they're prodding him along. Doc doesn't look like he's in any better shape—he must have put up quite a fight."

Mike leaned back against a tree, unable to look. "And Hannah?"

"She's the only one still on her feet."

Mike used his NVGs to zoom in enough to see the bruises on her cheek. She'd put up a fight and continued to resist their efforts to drag her along. The male prisoners were taken to the building with the rest of the crew, but the two guards on either side of Hannah were taking her down a different path.

As they dragged her, Mike didn't even need his imagination to guess what they planned to do. The two creeps began to play a game of hot potato with Hannah, pushing and shoving her between them, but she fought back.

She said something. The taller of the two slammed the butt of his automatic rifle into her gut, and she doubled over. The other, an eager fellow, removed his belt. He folded it in half and when she tried to stand upright, he slapped her across the face with such force that it knocked her to the ground.

Mike almost lost it. He was about to lose everything.

"I can take the shot," Nouri said, sighting down the scope.

What he left unsaid was that he'd be giving up their position and rescue plan—because they all knew it. Not all his men were in place yet. If Nouri took out the first Tango the second could send up an alarm to the lazy guards who hovered nearby. Hannah might even be caught in the crossfire.

Or Nouri could take out the first bad guy, maybe even the second and give her a chance to get free. But what about the other captives? If that was a man down there, even in a similar situation, there would be no debate. They'd stick to the plan.

Nouri waited for his call.

Mike hesitated. He never hesitated.

"The guy just dropped his pants," Itch murmured. "She's flat on her back. I think his intent is pretty clear."

Making it all that much harder for Mike to do what he had to do.

"Take the shot, or not?" Nouri asked again.

"Is she fighting back?" Mike asked, even though he knew the answer.

"No," Itch confirmed.

Because he'd taken all the fight out of her?

Mike took out his frustration on the nearest tree trunk. Dammit, he wasn't going to do her much good if he fell apart. But he didn't have a chance of rescuing her and the others if he got all his men killed.

"Not." The whispered word rang like a hollow point bullet in his ears. "Stick to the plan."

He'd been wrong to leave her behind. But what if *this* was the wrong call? He couldn't ask his men to risk their lives, but heaven help him, he couldn't stand by and watch her be raped, either.

"Two," he spoke to Ajax over the comm. "Plan B. I need to take care of some personal business." He scrambled down the hillside, toward Hannah.

"Mac, hold," Hazard advised.

Hazard, ever the voice of reason, stayed him.

Mike paused long enough for the SEAL to tell him the sane thing would be to stick to plan A. Insane would be to put the rescue of one over the rescue of eight.

But Itch's play-by-play began again, "She's just been playing possum. Calypso is kicking some serious ass."

Mike let himself take a peek as he continued to work his way down the incline. One of the Tangos had decided he needed a knife to get his point across to Hannah.

Using his own strength and the element of surprise against him, she'd used that knife on the man's partner, the guy with his pants down around his knees. Then she broke the knife welder's wrist.

He staggered back in pain, and she wheeled around and gave him a roundhouse kick to the chin. The man's head snapped back. For good measure, she picked up his weapon and hit him again with the butt end. Armed and more dangerous than ever, she dragged the bodies to the open space under the nearest building.

By the time Mike reached the camp, more men were heading toward her. She rolled under the hut. He came from the opposite side. He heard her soft intake of surprise and saw the knife blade an instant before recognition crossed her face.

He pressed his finger to his lips.

She nodded, and he stared into her eyes. The guard rounded the building and moved on to the next.

"All clear," Itch called through his mike.

"Copy," Mike whispered back. "Plan C. We're going to create a diversion inside the camp. Calypso and I will steal one of the trucks and disable the rest." He turned to her. "I don't have to ask if you're up for this."

Hannah went soft inside. The last thing she needed to do right now. McCaffrey wasn't acknowledging her as a woman, he was acknowledging her as a comrade.

Silently they used the spaces under the buildings to get closer to the trucks. There was more activity at this end of camp. At one point they had to enter one of the darkened buildings.

A map-strewn table was covered with important-looking documents. McCaffrey snapped a couple of quick pictures and gathered up some of the papers, spreading the rest around to make it look untouched.

A whispered warning in his comm alerted McCaffrey, and he alerted Hannah just as steps mounted the stairs. They hustled into a back room. McCaffrey climbed out the window, signaled all-clear, then hauled her after him.

They could see the trucks from where they were. Hannah didn't know how they'd get to them with so many men standing around. She ducked when a loud boom at the opposite end of camp sent the guerrillas running to see what was happening. Two of the men were instructed to stay behind.

McCaffrey signaled for her to stay put as he

sneaked up behind guard number one and made quick work of him. He wound his way around the back of the truck toward the other guard.

The guy made a sudden move away from the tailgate and toward McCaffrey's position.

Hannah stepped into view. "I need some help here." She waved at the guard. He pointed his weapon and motioned her away from the truck. McCaffrey stepped up behind him with his K-bar, and seconds later the guard slumped to the ground. She saw a flash of regret in McCaffrey's eyes—one he probably hadn't wanted her to see.

But then he became the brisk professional once again. He searched the bodies for keys. None. "We're going to have to hot-wire it."

He rigged two of the three trucks with C-4, then they scrambled into the third. Since they needed quick over pretty McCaffrey reached for the screwdriver from his web gear.

In the instant he would have ripped into the ignition, Hannah flipped down the sun visor, and the keys fell in his lap. The look on his face was priceless. She decided not to tell him she'd seen her driver stow the keys there.

He drove at breakneck speed toward the building where the crew was being held. Out in the open they drew attention. And gunfire.

Hannah fired back.

"Take the wheel," McCaffrey shouted as he skidded to a stop. He opened his door, firing cover as his men dragged the injured to the truck. She got a quick head count. They were leaving with two extra. Either the SEALs had taken prisoners or they'd rescued hostages.

Fired on from all directions, Hannah drove through the maze of bullets and men and around the two remaining trucks toward the gate while the SEALs fired back. A second explosion rocked the camp as the trucks exploded, stopping at least half of their pursuers.

Hannah swerved to avoid hitting a man in the road. From the corner of her eye, she watched him raise his weapon.

Mike took him out. "Let's not stop for any more pedestrians," he said. "Or the gate."

Hannah floored it, crashing through the gate in a tangle of razor wire and vine.

CHAPTER FOURTEEN

NAVAL AIR STATION NORTH ISLAND
Coronado, California

SO MUCH FOR CAMARADERIE. She was getting her ass chewed in debriefing. And McCaffrey was doing most of the gnawing. So it surprised her when he paused long enough to pour a cup a coffee, took his usual sip, then handed it to her without a word.

Cream and sugar, just the way she liked it. He preferred his own gully wash black, which he proceeded to pour for himself.

For some reason the sip didn't bother her this time, perhaps because it was the only kindness he'd shown her in the past twenty-four hours since they'd climbed aboard the Seahawks and then boarded their respective planes for home.

The injured had been treated on Basilan and released. Then Spence had been flow on to Manila for further medical attention.

Hannah studied the tight lines around McCaffrey's mouth as she drank her coffee. Still no mention of the baby.

But this was hardly the time or place to talk about

their daughter. There was one intel officer for every able-bodied man in the room. With her two gunships crews, the four fire teams and the two Filipino soldiers they'd rescued, that meant seventeen intel officers and at least forty personnel in all. She couldn't keep the count straight anymore.

The guy assigned to her, a captain, was relentless. On top of that, Admiral Bell had questions, and the captain assigned to debrief McCaffrey seemed to be comparing notes, because he had questions for her, too.

It didn't help any that she and McCaffrey had resorted to name-calling, which had resulted in a shouting match between the two of them. He'd actually called her a liar when the admiral interrogated her about the death of Sergeant Wray.

So now a shrink and a Bible thumper had been added to the mix. She didn't know the chaplain's purpose, other than to keep their swearing to a minimum, but she definitely didn't like the shrink.

"So how long have you two been sleeping together?" the female officer asked.

You could have heard a pin drop in the room that a moment ago had been buzzing with questions and answers.

"Excuse me?" Hannah hated the way her voice cracked, that she'd been the one to speak up at all *and* that Dr. What's-Her-Name was able to write a paragraph of notes after those two little words.

"Just curious as to why Commander McCaffrey feels the need to protect you."

Mac mumbled something about the line of questioning.

"Because he's insane," Hannah said, hoping to deflect some of the attention from herself. "He feels the need to protect everyone."

Great, now the woman was writing a book.

"Let's go over this again," the admiral said. "One last time. Who killed Sergeant Wray?"

"I shot him twice to the head—"

"I shot him—" McCaffrey gestured toward the pictures on the table as proof.

"Nouri and Itch back up your story, Mac, but I've got five SEALs and two crewmen who say they heard four rounds fired."

McCaffrey swore under his breath. "She's a lousy shot. She missed by a mile."

"I did not miss—"

"So, Mac, you're changing your story?" the admiral asked.

"Lieutenant Commander Stanton suffered a head injury. Her memory is still a little fuzzy." He stared her down, daring her to deny it. "I killed Sergeant Wray."

"He did not—"

The admiral cut her off with a wave of his hand. "Mac, final word, for the record. Whose ass belongs in that hot seat?"

"Mine," he said with conviction.

"So be it," the admiral said with a total lack of conviction. He turned to the armed Marines at the door. "After the debriefing Commander McCaffrey is to be confined to NAVCOMBRIG *Miramar* to await a hearing on the matter—"

"Hell, Warren—" McCaffrey stalked toward the admiral "—where is it you think I'm running to? You could've just confined me to quarters." He surrendered to the Marines in defiance. "As far as I'm concerned this debriefing is over."

"Stop!" Hannah couldn't take any more. This was so wrong. So out of control. He was lying to protect her. Somehow he'd convinced himself this was the right thing to do. How could she convince everyone in the room otherwise?

She looked to Mac for help, the last place she expected to find it, and pleaded with her eyes. His eyes softened, he even smiled. Then he opened his sarcastic mouth. "Don't worry, I don't expect you to wait for me while I'm in Leavenworth."

Excited Tagalog broke out in the corner where the two Filipinos were being questioned through an interpreter. "They're saying al-Ayman's men killed Sergeant Wray."

The admiral lifted his hands in surrender. "Let's hear it."

"Wray and another man. Perez—" the interpreter stopped talking to listen "—were with their unit. They say that is not a picture of Sergeant Wray. Wray was tortured and killed because he would not give up the—" he repeated something in Tagalog, listened, then translated "—the daily codes, the passwords."

"They held out as long as they could, but they were also tortured. Together they came up with the idea of giving up the password, but the previous day's to throw off al-Ayman. They feel much shame for their act of cowardice, therefore they did not speak up, but they will not allow an innocent man to go to jail. They are certain the man in the picture was one of their captors."

"Would someone find out who the hell this guy is," the admiral demanded, picking up the photo and flinging it at the nearest intel officer.

Not just one, but several officers left the room in a hurry.

"Am I off the hook?" McCaffrey asked Admiral Bell.

"I'd say you're dangling, Mac. But in the case of Sergeant Wray, you're off the hook, *for now.* However, there's still the matter of Lieutenant Commander Stanton disobeying direct orders—"

"Misunderstanding," McCaffrey said.

"Really? Okay," the admiral agreed. "Now I'm interested to know how you're going to explain away the crash of not one, but two of Uncle Sam's multi-million-dollar aircraft. Go ahead, tell me how you crashed both helicopters, Mac."

"I ran out of batteries."

"You ran out of batteries? And that caused the crash of two helicopters?"

"We had to ditch excess weight on the run. We couldn't stop to get a satellite uplink. The batteries in my two-way were weak. The connection was weak. I ordered Lieutenant Commander Stanton to abort. I guess she didn't hear me."

"It was my call," Hannah spoke up, sick and tired of him trying to cover for her. "I did what any *man* would have done in the same situation. You were under fire, and I went in after your ass. Just admit that, please. I don't care if you think I was right or wrong, just admit that it was my call."

"I call it from the ground," he argued.

"Well, I call it from the air. And we were in the air."

"I ordered you to abort, Commander."

"Is this about the baby?"

Mac went pale, his jaw tightened.

He'd meant the pickup, of course, but somewhere in her mind, the lines had blurred. Beneath their argument about the mission was the real one. The personal one.

The admiral ordered the room cleared. "Not you two. You are going to sit there until you can go twenty minutes without an argument."

WHEN MIKE GOT MAD, he got silent.

His brooding filled the debriefing room. He checked his watch again. He'd sit out his twenty minutes in silence or until hell froze over—whichever came first.

He refused to look at Hannah, to speak to her or to acknowledge her in any way when she tried to talk to him. He had no doubt that if he opened his mouth right now the admiral would add another twenty minutes to their time-out.

Her comment had been unprofessional and un-called-for. Totally out of character for Hannah. And nobody's business but theirs. As if he would have ever asked her to abort his child. Hell, he might have done exactly that if he'd had the chance. Who could say how he would have reacted?

All that mattered was how he reacted *now*—and from this moment forward. He *was* the father of a five-month-old baby girl. He could finally think about all that meant. He kept up an impatient tapping of his toe, stole a glance at Hannah, then looked away. She stared down at the tabletop, head in her hands, fingers tangled through ratty curls.

Dammit. She'd better not be crying.

Debriefing wasn't just about answering questions. It was about getting out all those feelings they didn't allow themselves to have in the field. Letting go of all of those bottled-up emotions so that they didn't screw up a guy's head. He'd glossed over, even taken the blame for mistakes made by his men before, but he'd never lied in debriefing.

He'd never held so much of what he was feeling back, either. No wonder the admiral had wanted to bring him up on charges.

Of course no one on his squad had ever turned to him and said "You have a daughter."

He had a daughter and her name was Fallon.

She'd been conceived in a Reno, Nevada, hotel room. With a woman he'd been engaged in foreplay with for four years prior to that. There was no other way to put it. They'd been hot for each other, and keeping that at bay, during all those training days in the desert just made them hotter.

At the first opportunity—hell, maybe not the first opportunity—but certainly the first opportunity where they weren't both on duty and in uniform, they'd acted on that attraction. He'd gone to bed thinking, yeah, this is kind of nice. And he'd woke thinking, not kind of nice, exactly what he wanted. A woman who understood him. A woman who wouldn't have any unrealistic exceptions. The perfect woman for him.

But nowhere in that equation was there a baby.

In the wee hours of the morning, he'd reached for that last condom on the nightstand.

"I'm on the pill," she'd said.

"I accept that invitation." He'd rolled her beneath him, and she'd threaded her fingers through his. That last condom had stayed in their clasped hands. He hadn't even broken eye contact to kiss her, just eased into her and rocked until they'd both exploded.

They weren't inexperienced teenagers.

They had made a conscious choice.

They knew the risks. And the consequences.

"Time's up," Mike said to whoever was listening in, either through the speaker system or from behind the two-way mirror. "I'm outta here."

He headed for the door, pausing only long enough to hold it open for her. She didn't say anything, not even a polite little thank-you, simply ducked into the ladies' room while he headed for the exit.

The debriefing was where the mission ended, and the real world began. On this mission Hannah had forever changed his world.

Squinting against the sun, he plucked his sunglasses from the breast pocket of his BDU. Putting them on, he noticed Hannah's mother standing among the reunited wives and sweethearts and their servicemen. And there was the sister in charge of the baby buggy. Not the big clunky one from last time, but one that folded up like an umbrella when it was closed.

He walked straight up to them and without so much as a by-your-leave, ma'am, he hunkered down to have a good look at his kid.

His eyes. His hair. Both brown.

Some called his eyes hazel because they changed from light to dark, depending on his mood. Did hers do that, too?

His smile. Crooked.

Maybe he'd still demand a blood test just to piss Hannah off. His daughter had Hannah's nose. He could only hope she wasn't inclined to stick it up in the air like her mother.

The baby threw her pacifier at him. Definitely her mother's daughter. The soother hit the dirt, and he pocketed it. She reached for it, latching on to his finger instead, then trying to bring his finger to her mouth. She had a good grip, and her nails were so tiny and paper-thin he was in awe of them.

She had all ten fingers and all ten toes from what he could count when she wasn't kicking at him. She looked healthy enough and seemed happy enough.

He picked up her lost sock from the ground and tucked it beside her. Then he reached in to unstrap her.

"Mac—" Sam started to protest, but he cut her off with a look, a look that conveyed his newfound knowledge.

The baby had grown in the past month and a half. What was she now—four? Almost five months? He liked the solid feel of her in his arms. "I'm going to be taking my daughter for a walk," he announced to the two women.

Samantha turned over the stroller without hesitation. "Where should I tell Hannah she can find you?"

"She'll find me." He started for the hangar in the distance, looking over his shoulder as Hannah headed straight for him.

It took her a full minute to catch up. "Where do you think you're taking her, Mike?" He could hear the panic in her voice.

"To your office." He let Hannah enter the building first. Evident relief washed over her as they stepped inside her office. She took Fallon from him. And he let her.

"Look how big!" she cooed. "Mommy missed you."

Hands tucked under his arms, Mike stood back and watched the exchange between his daughter and his daughter's mother.

Fallon started to fuss. Turning her little body into a corkscrew, his daughter reached for him. Hannah looked so distraught he kept his hands to himself.

"I know Mommy smells like dirty socks," she said.

It wasn't the sweetest analogy, but an accurate one. They both smelled as if they'd crawled out of the jungle, because of course they had.

"I'm sorry, Mike."

"You should have told me."

"I didn't know how." Tears glistened in her eyes.

"If you're going to cry, find another shoulder, Stanton, or suck it up." He'd meant to be cruel. He didn't want her to shed those tears. If she started crying, he'd have no choice but to forgive her.

Heaven help him, he didn't hate her.

He only wanted to.

She took a deep breath, holding back all those tears and anything else she might be feeling, and stood her ground. "You can hate me. I don't blame you. But we don't expect or want anything from you."

"*We* as in you and the baby? Where do I fit into this? What about what I want?" he demanded. "I never pegged you for selfish, Han. I guess I was wrong about a lot of things."

"That's not fair. I didn't have the opportunity—"

"The way I see it you let a hell of a lot of opportunities pass you by."

"Then what do you want?" she asked him point-blank.

"I don't know what I want. I'm only just now getting used to the idea of being a father. I never wanted—" He stopped himself short. Before he said something he'd never be able to take back.

"A kid? To be a father?" she finished for him.

"I would have liked some say in the matter, yes. There are things we should have consulted on. Family histories for one. Names for another. Fallon is the name of a place I don't particularly care for. I don't have the kind of lifestyle to support a family—"

"No one's asking you to commit, McCaffrey. As far as I'm concerned, you're off the hook." She purposely parroted the admiral. "Walk away with a clear conscience. You have my permission."

"What about my daughter's permission? What are you going to tell her? I'm the guy that was good at leaving and not so good at sticking around? You're sure as hell trying hard enough to push me away. Were you ever even on the pill?"

"You think I tricked you for your swimmers?"

"I don't know what to think. You're standing there telling me the two of you are going to be fine without me." That had come out too sharply. The baby started to cry. Mike pinched the bridge of his nose. He'd once told Hannah any day with no bullets flying by was a good day. Well, this was a pretty damn good day, and he didn't want to ruin it with anger and pettiness.

Hannah was the mother of his child.

Did anything else really matter? He couldn't change the past. She should have told him about the pregnancy, about the baby. She didn't. But he could shoulder his share of blame for that. Now that he knew, there was no doubt in his mind about where they'd go from here. "Can you take tomorrow off? It's Friday. How about an extra long weekend? Monday is Labor Day. I'd like to take the baby home to see my folks."

"This weekend?" She'd pulled a clean pacifier from somewhere and was bouncing the baby on her hip. "We just got back. It's not really convenient—"

"You owe me."

"Okay," she sighed heavily, "I'll make the necessary arrangements to take the time off."

"Thank you."

"Are you sure you know what you're getting yourself into, Mike? A daughter is a lifetime commitment. Her lifetime as well as yours."

"We can drive to Vegas tonight if you'd like or wait until tomorrow and get married in Reno. It's just a hop, skip and a jump across the state line from the folks."

"I didn't mean it was a lifetime commitment for *us*."

"This isn't about you or me. This is about our daughter and doing the right thing for her."

"Getting married is not the right thing."

"I'm not going to argue the finer points of illegitimacy."

"Good, then don't."

"You got to choose the first name. I'm choosing the last."

"Your name is on the birth certificate, Mike. Fallon Rose Stanton-McCaffrey. She's already a McCaffrey if that's what she wants."

He felt humbled by that. But still not satisfied. "Will you quit arguing me in circles, woman. We have a baby. We're getting married."

"That's not even close to a proposal. And in any case I don't accept. You can't force me to marry you. I'm not convinced—"

He grabbed her and pulled her to him. "Let me convince you," he said, swallowing her protest. His mouth came down hard on her softer, surprise-parted lips.

He had to be careful not to crush the baby in his full-on assault so he only held Hannah by putting a hand on the back of her head. But she wasn't even trying to escape his kiss.

He tangled his hand in that red hair of hers. He let her feel how badly he needed her, how badly he needed to make things right. She tasted so sweet. So right. He didn't even know he wasn't shaking with anger, but with fear, until he realized just how much he had to lose if he let her say no.

Her hand slipped up to ease the tension at the

base of his neck, but there was only one thing that would release his lower-body tension. He wanted her to touch him there before another kind of fear and doubt set in—that maybe she was right. He wasn't cut out for this.

Fallon dropped her soother in their love nest and wailed. Nothing like a kid crying in your ear to douse the flame. Hannah backed away, comforting their crying daughter. "I'm still not convinced that means you'll stick around."

CHAPTER FIFTEEN

"HANNAH, IS THAT YOU?" her mother called out from the kitchen.

Hannah held her daughter in one arm and her seabag in the other. Her mother had left the keys to the Lexus and a discreet note about catching a ride home with JJ at the yeoman's desk.

"Oh, honey, it's so good to see you," her mother said, getting up from the table to hug her. "You know Captain Loring, don't you?" She sniffed the air around Hannah. "Oh, my goodness, what is that smell?"

"It's me, Mother."

"Give me the baby," her mother demanded, taking Fallon. "Go upstairs and shower and change."

What with the crash, the debriefing and the confrontation with McCaffrey, she wasn't in the mood to give up control of any other aspect of her life.

She took Fallon back and retreated to her bedroom. She didn't even care that it was her mother's furnishings throughout the house and not her own, until she found her things stored in the nursery and in her bedroom. They hadn't even bothered to put together her bed. Everything was just leaning up against the wall. She wanted to cry.

But she was so dead-on-her-feet tired, sleep sounded better.

She should have been mad at McCaffrey for daring to kiss her in anger, but the man had been trembling in her arms, which made her putty in his.

She changed the baby in the Portacrib, then let her play there while she made enough room to drop the king-size mattress to the floor.

Then Hannah stripped, put on a clean T-shirt and collapsed on top of the mattress. "Mommy's home."

For now.

"SEAN MICHAEL MCCAFFREY!"

Only his mother could make him feel guilty just by using his given name. Sean was a name he despised and hadn't used since kindergarten, which was when he'd told his teacher his name was Mike and the name had stuck.

The doorbell rang.

"Could you hold on a sec, Ma?" Mike switched the phone to his left ear and dug in his back pocket for his wallet. "Gotta get the door," he said, walking toward it.

"You haven't called home in more than a year and you put me on hold? Not even a call on Mother's Day, Michael. Or Father's Day, your father says. What kind of son did we raise?"

"A hungry one." He opened the door to the deliveryman from Wong's Chinese. He took the brown bag, paid the man, including a hefty tip for the rush, and closed the door.

"I suppose there's no food in the house. Would it hurt you to go to the grocery store once in a while?"

"There's no food in the house, because I'm never here."

"He's not eating," she said to his father.

"Ma, I'm eating."

"I bet you're all skin and bones."

"I'm thirty-five, not sixteen."

"I know how old you are, Michael. I gave birth to you, remember? Do I ever forget your birthday?"

"I sent a card. Mother's Day, too."

"But you didn't call. And whoever heard of electronic cards? I had to have your sister print it out on fancy paper to prove to everyone my boy doesn't forget his mother's birthday."

Everyone being the busybodies in her church group he was sure. It had taken a lot of effort and planning for him to set his computer to send cards on birthdays and holidays, to pay his bills on time. Why couldn't she give him credit for that?

Wasn't it the thought that counted?

He thought about his family all the time. He just had to set reminders so they'd know it when he couldn't tell them himself.

"Are you through giving me a hard time?"

"You know we love you, Michael. That's why we

give you a hard time. Now your father wants to know if you're coming home for our anniversary dinner?"

"Uh, that's what I called to talk to you about."

"Oh, Michael—"

"It's not that. I'll be there. It's just— I'm bringing someone with me—"

"He's bringing a date," she said to his father. "You're father says good, it's about time—"

"Not a date, Ma. I have a little girl. A daughter. Her name is Fallon. She's five months old."

"Oh, Michael…"

Thirty-five years old, and he still held his breath, awaiting their reaction, their approval. There was a long pause as his mother relayed the news to his father.

Then his father came on the line. "Fallon's a good Irish name, son."

"I had nothing to do with naming her. I just found out about this myself."

"I see." His father said a lot with those two words. "*This* being the baby and all? Does this baby, *your* baby, have a mother?"

"Hannah," he said, looking down at his forgotten dinner.

"Her name's Hannah," his father said to his mother.

His mother took the line again. "How come we've never heard mention of her before this?"

"You'll meet her this weekend. Look, we can stay in a motel—"

"You won't be staying in any motel. You'll be

staying right here, the three of you. He wants to stay in a motel," she said to his father. "Your father wants to know what Hannah's father does for a living and if we'll be meeting her folks before the wedding?"

"There isn't going to be a wedding."

MIKE PULLED UP in front of Hannah's house at 0500. She must have been waiting for him because she carried the baby outside before he reached the door. His baby. Mike was glad to see she'd packed light, only one suitcase.

"I'll get that," he offered, taking it from her and heading back toward his Jeep. She didn't follow.

"No baby of mine is riding in a vehicle with a roll bar."

"Point taken." He grabbed his gear and hauled both back to her Lexus. She popped her trunk.

"The rest of Fallon's things are inside by the door. I'll buckle her into her car seat."

Mike dutifully trod up the walk. Inside he found diaper bag, baby-gym, umbrella stroller, Portacrib, another suitcase and an overnight bag the size of his. He loaded up and hauled it outside. "I did say just the weekend right?"

"You've never traveled with a baby before."

"I've never had a baby before."

"Point taken," she said. "Don't put the diaper bag in the trunk. I'll need that here in the back seat. The overnight bag, too."

"Anything else?" he asked before closing the lid.

"That's it," she said, getting in on the driver's side. "Oh, would you mind leaving your keys with Sammy? We only have the one car."

"You really know how to hurt a guy." He took a deep, almost comical breath and walked his keys to the front door where he exchanged a few pleasantries with Hannah's sister.

Mike rode shotgun. A bit different than last time—he wasn't toting any weapons, and she wasn't speeding through the gates of a terrorist training camp. Yeah, today was a pretty damn good day.

"That everything?" he asked.

She ran through some sort of a mental checklist. "I think we're all set." She put the keys in the ignition and started the car.

"Nice hardtop. I'd like to take a ride with top down sometime," he commented, keeping their conversation on neutral ground.

"Not with the baby."

He hadn't meant right now, but let the comment slide.

"If you give me the address I can punch it into the GPS," she offered.

"I know where we're going." He'd made the trip often enough. "It's about a ten-hour trip. How much does one of these things run anyway?"

"Seventy-five."

"*Thousand?* That's more than I paid for my house in Imperial Beach ten years ago." He gave in to the gadget and plugged his parents' address into the GPS system. Who the hell paid 75K for a car? "Nine hours, fifty-three minutes. Six hundred and fifty-one miles."

"If you say so." She sounded doubtful.

"Petrone pays that well?" Now there's a name he never thought he'd bring up in conversation again.

"He does."

"I take it the one weekend a month, two weeks a year, warrior gig isn't for the extra cash?"

"I like to fly."

"You must have taken a pretty big pay cut when you were activated."

"I did."

Come on. He was trying here. "What exactly is your net worth?"

She gave him a look, a look that said none-of-your-beeswax.

"An estimate. Mid-six?"

"Higher."

"*Seven figures!* Why are you even in the reserves? Why don't you just stay home with the baby?"

"Why don't you stay home with her? You make less money than I do."

Ouch! "Not right now I don't. Take the next right," he said. "Anyway, you know I can't." Neither of them could. Resigning during conflict might be interpreted as an act of cowardice.

"You don't do it for the money, Mike. Why would you assume I do?"

"That's not what I meant." He glanced over the back seat at their daughter. Buckled in behind the driver, in a rear-facing car seat, all he could see were her hands batting at the toy hanging overhead. He reached over and put his hand on her head, smoothing back her hair. "It would just be nice if one of us could. That's all I was saying."

Fallon twisted against her restraint trying to get a better look at him. She dropped her pacifier and started bawling. He plugged her back in.

Deciding to drop the subject before he found himself in hot water, Mike fiddled with the satellite radio. "What do you like to listen to?" Restless, he scanned the preset buttons, then flipped through her CD collection. "Movie soundtracks? You collect movie soundtracks?"

"What's wrong with that?"

"*What Women Want*," he read, then turned it over, "*Bitch* and *Mack the Knife*. I'm not even going to ask. Do you have anything else? Classical music for babies," he answered his own question. "Turn left on Coronado Cays."

Hannah pulled over. "Would you like to drive?"

"I thought you'd never ask."

They opened their respective doors and played musical chairs, except Hannah got in the back seat with Fallon.

"Now I'm your chauffeur? With the money you make, I guess that sounds about right."

"Somebody has to keep her entertained or she's

going to sleep right through the whole trip and be up all night."

What about him? Who was going to keep him entertained?

He put in a CD and sang along with Meredith Brooks about female empowerment.

"Just drive," Hannah said with laughter in her voice.

He stole a glance in the rearview mirror. "It's good to see you smiling again, Han."

"I was thinking the same thing about you, McCaffrey."

"ARE WE THERE YET?" Hannah asked, rousing herself when the car rolled to a stop. She'd moved to the front passenger seat to let Fallon nap before meeting her grandparents. She'd been dozing on and off herself because McCaffrey wouldn't give up control of the wheel.

Twelve hours into their road trip, and he was no longer smiling. Hannah couldn't help it; she wanted to laugh out loud, he was being so darn surly. He'd underestimated the number of stops required when traveling with a baby.

"Not much farther," he said. "Half hour. Hannah—"

"Where are we?" In a parking lot. She read the neon sign. "The Last Chance Chapel. Nevada? We're in Nevada?"

"Any chance you've changed your mind?" He

gripped the steering wheel with his left hand, his knuckles almost white.

"What exactly did you tell your parents about us?"

Understandably, she was already nervous about meeting them and this didn't make it any easier. At their last rest stop, she'd changed Fallon into a new outfit then put her down so she'd awaken at her cutest.

"They're a bit old-fashioned. But I didn't concoct some fairy tale, if that's what you're getting at."

"Good. Because I'm not getting married in the Divorce Capital of the World at the Last Chance Chapel."

"So that's a maybe?"

No! That's what she should have said, Hannah decided some twenty minutes later, still trying to recover from the shock of his confident pronouncement.

Headed southwest now, and far away from Reno, though not far enough for her, he turned down a dirt road at about seven-thirty in the evening. The sun set in amber waves over the beautiful Sierra Nevada mountain range. They'd passed Lake Tahoe and newer luxury homes along the way, but the rambling white farmhouse up ahead felt like a real home. Horses trotted up to the fence next to the barn, and three men and two boys standing around the upturned cab of an eighteen-wheeler waved.

Two barking hounds ran out to the tree-lined

driveway to meet them—straight out of a Norman Rockwell picture.

Mike slowed to avoid hitting the dogs. Honking a warning or a welcome, he rolled down his window and waved back to the men who headed their way. The back door opened on the women and more children filed out.

As the small battalion advanced on them, Mike got out of the car. "Hey, Jewel. Hey, Ruby." He pushed the dogs back before they could climb in all over the leather car seats.

Hannah was slower, less certain about getting out of the car. The dogs sensed her hesitation and jumped her.

"Down," Mike ordered, and they obeyed.

"Michael." A woman Hannah assumed was his mother folded him into her arms.

Then he got several more hugs and kisses from his sisters before the big redheaded man in bib overalls wiped his grease-stained hands and pulled Mike into a bear hug. "Welcome home, son."

"Mike's home! Mike's home!" An adult she'd mistaken for a child threw his arms around Mike's middle.

"Hannah, this is my brother, Buddy." He introduced his brother while knuckling his towhead. Buddy stood about five feet, two inches compared to Mike's six feet, two.

"I'm Buddy," he enunciated carefully in a surprisingly deep voice. He held out his hand.

"Buddy, it's nice to meet you. I'm Hannah." They shook hands.

"Hannah and Mike have a baby," Buddy said. His grin got big and his eyes closed to tiny slits. The smile lit up his face.

"Yes, we do," she answered, hoping it didn't sound as if she was talking down to him. He must be around twenty-five, and he had peach fuzz on his chin. "Her name is Fallon. Would you like to meet her?" Hannah opened the back door.

"Mike?" Buddy demanded. "Does your baby have Down Syndrome like me?"

THE SUBJECT HADN'T come up when Mike had talked to his folks. But he knew it had to have been on their minds, and judging from Buddy's question, the topic of dinner conversation around the McCaffrey household. Buddy was a perfect mimic.

Mike broke the awkward silence. "No, Bud, Fallon doesn't have Down Syndrome."

"That's good, Mike," Buddy said with the pragmatic wisdom of the very innocent. "'Cause we're going to love her no matter what."

"That's right," Mike agreed, hugging Buddy to his side. "We're gonna love her."

Dammit. His eyes felt like a sandstorm had just blown in from the desert. Every time he got to this altitude, his sinuses acted up. The animals didn't help. Neither did that knot in his gut that had just relaxed with relief.

His daughter was perfect. He'd jumped a hurdle without even realizing he'd come to it. She'd have been perfect and he'd have loved her no matter what. He could let go of that old fear now, couldn't he?

Where did that leave him exactly, now that he'd found the courage to love unconditionally? Maybe he'd always had that capability.

"Everybody," he said to his family, "this is Hannah and our daughter, Fallon. Hannah," he squeezed her shoulder, offering his reassurance. "This is everybody. Don't worry, you'll catch on. We won't throw the names at you all at once. You've met Buddy. Here's my mom and dad."

"Mr. and Mrs. McCaffrey," Hannah held Fallon upright to show her off.

"None of that Mr. and Mrs.," his father said. "We answer to Shamus and Maudie, but Mom and Dad will do if you're so inclined. You've made an old man happy giving a fine Irish name like Fallon to a McCaffrey. Now bring the boy to heel so I can die a happy man. He's a lack-brain if he hasn't proposed at least a dozen times already."

"Shamus, you said you wouldn't say anything. Never you mind, Hannah. Don't let an old man's folly scare you off. Make the boy propose another dozen times to make sure he's worthy. That's what I did with this one here. Now let me at that sweet grandbaby." His mother took Fallon right from Hannah's arms.

HANNAH STIFLED A YAWN.

"Hannah, you look tired after your long trip. We shouldn't have kept you up so late," Maude said, putting an end to the conversation. "I see you brought a portable crib? I already set up the old crib in the guest room. I put you both in there. That's all right, isn't it?"

"Of course, thank you." Hannah was used to sleeping in the same room with Fallon and actually preferred it.

Mike's mother carried Fallon upstairs and Hannah followed. "Sean Michael McCaffrey," she called back downstairs, "get off your duff and bring the bags with you." She turned to the left. "This used to be the girls' room. But after all the kids were gone, I converted it into a guest/sewing room. There's a connecting bathroom and on the other side is the boys' room. But don't worry, Buddy won't bother you. You can lock the bathroom door, and he'll use the one downstairs…"

Maude continued her nervous rambling, and Hannah realized the woman was eager for her approval and some of her own nervousness disappeared. She was eager to please Mike's family, as well. And although they didn't seem to have much else in common they did have that.

Mike stepped into the room to drop off her bags.

Maude turned to face him. "Your father and I have decided to keep an open mind about the whole situation. You're both mature adults. You have a child together. And we see no reason why you shouldn't be allowed to share a bedroom in our home."

Had *both* meant her and Mike, not her and Fallon?

"Ma—"

"It's okay. We know how these modern relationships work. We're just so happy for you and we're happy to have Hannah and Fallon as part of our family. Okay, then. I've rattled on long enough. I know you're both tired. Sleep tight, dears." She kissed Fallon's cheek then handed her over to Hannah on the way out.

Mike closed the door. "You okay with this? I can explain things to her—"

"Don't make a fuss. It doesn't have to be that complicated. As long as you don't mind sleeping on the floor." Hannah tossed one of the pillows to the side of the bed, then turned her attention to the crib. "This is a beautiful piece of furniture. How old would you say it is?"

"At least thirty-five years."

Hannah ran her hand lovingly across the top. Mike had slept here as a baby. Of course the bedding would have to go. Shifting Fallon on her hip, she put the bedding on a chair. "Do you think these slats are more than six inches apart?"

"Maybe." He stopped fixing his makeshift bed on the floor and reached for his vest pocket, but didn't find it because he wasn't wearing his web gear.

There was a soft knock on the door, followed by it opening. "I brought you some—" Maude stood in the doorway with a load of clean towels. "Is something wrong?" she asked, staring at the pillow and blankets on the floor.

"I tried to tell you—"

"Mike hurt his back rappelling from a helicopter during our last training exercise. He needs to sleep on a hard surface for a while."

"Oh, Michael," his mother said with some relief. "The things you get yourself into. I'll just put these towels in the bathroom."

Mike shot Hannah a grateful look.

"I hope your back is better soon," Maude said as she was leaving. "Don't forget your bag is out here in the hall. Sleep in tomorrow as long as you like. I'm making pancakes."

Hannah got the sneaking suspicion that even though Mrs. M. played along she didn't quite believe their deception. Hannah had done it for Mike just as much as for his mother. He seemed to need his parents to believe everything was fine and dandy with their little family—not that they were really a family.

"I think if you open up the top right drawer of that sewing table you'll find a tape measure," he said.

She laid Fallon down in the crib and opened the drawer to find the tape measure. "They're right at six, but I think that's okay. I had to make sure the baby's head couldn't get caught between the slats," she said before he could ask. "And quilts are suffocation hazards."

"Good to know for future reference," he said. "Mind if I use the bathroom while you're putting her down?"

"Go ahead."

He grabbed his bag from the hall.

Leaving Fallon playing with her toes in the crib, Hannah put her suitcase on an old dining-room chair that served as the sewing chair. She dug through for a clean sleeper for the baby and her own pj's.

By the time she'd changed the baby and got her settled in for the night, Mike had emerged from the bathroom. She turned down the light on her way, and he settled onto the floor.

The hardwood wouldn't be comfortable.

Served him right for keeping secrets. "Good night, Sean."

CHAPTER SIXTEEN

HANNAH SLEPT in until 0800. The very first thing she realized was that Fallon was still sleeping. Of course her daughter had had a long drive and a loving family to wear her out. For her own part, Hannah found the McCaffrey clan a bit overwhelming.

Mike had already tidied up his bedroll and left the room. She wanted a shower, but she wasn't sure if Fallon would continue to sleep through it.

Opening the hall door, Hannah found Buddy right outside, wearing headphones and jamming to the overloud tunes coming from his CD player. He saw her and smiled.

She smiled back. "Buddy, Buddy," she had to repeat his name several times before he slipped off one earpiece. "Could you go get Mike?"

"Hi, Fallon's mom."

"Hi," she said back. "Could you go get Mike for me, please?"

"Mike's not here."

"Not here? Where'd he go?" Had his pager gone off?

"He's not here," Buddy repeated.

"Okay," she said.

"Buddy?" Maude called up the stairs. "You're not bothering Hannah, are you?"

"No, I'm waiting. I'm waiting for Hannah and the baby to get up."

"Well, you come downstairs. And don't bother them."

"He's not bothering us, Maude," Hannah called down. "I was just wondering if Mike was around."

Maude climbed the stairs to the landing so they were at least visible to each other. "They went into town for some truck parts."

"Do you know when he'll be back?"

"What is it you need, dear?" Maude got to the point.

"I just wanted to take a shower. Fallon's still asleep—" amazing with all the shouting back and forth "—and I thought he could listen for her, in case she wakes up."

"Just leave the bedroom door cracked and I'll hear her from the kitchen." Hannah must have let her glance slide to Buddy because Maude said, "He's not going to bother the baby."

"Don't bother the baby. No, no, no. Don't bother Hannah and the baby."

Somehow, bless Buddy, that didn't sound very reassuring. Hannah tried to figure a polite way out of her dilemma when Maude ushered Buddy downstairs with her. Relieved, Hannah left both the bedroom and bathroom doors ajar, just in case. Stripping, she hurried through her shower, keeping one ear tuned to the baby.

Turning off the water, she opened the shower door, reached for a towel and screamed.

"Bang." A two-foot cowboy aimed his toy gun and shot her. "Bang."

"Out!" Hannah demanded, snagging the nearest towel and wrapping herself in it. The baby started crying. The door to the "boys' room" slammed on girlish giggles, leaving only one escape route for little Tex.

"What's going on here?" Mike asked from the bedroom.

"Bang!" He shot at Mike and tried to get past him.

Mike picked his nephew up off the ground, gave him a pat on the behind, then set him down. "Go find your mother!"

The boy ran out of the room. Hannah stood there in her towel. Fallon had stopped crying the minute she'd heard her father's voice.

Mike locked the bedroom door behind his nephew. "Guess I should have warned you. Big families have no respect for privacy. Gotta lock *both* doors." He grinned at her.

She moved to the closet and rifled through the few items she'd brought with her. "I wish you'd mentioned the anniversary dinner. I have nothing to wear…"

When he didn't say anything, she turned to find

him staring at her. She pulled the towel more se-
curely around her.

"I'm just trying to imagine you pregnant."

Becoming even more self-conscious, she tucked
a damp curl behind her ear. "Fat and awkward," she
said, trying to break the tension.

"Show me," he said, already moving across the
room. "Show me the body you've been trying so
hard to hide."

"I'm not going to stand here and flash you my
stretch mar—"

He parted the towel to caress the natural curves
of her hips and breasts. "I don't see any stretch
marks," he lied.

They were faint and getting fainter, but they were
there, though his touch went a long way in making
her believe anything that came from his lips. He bent
to suckle at her breast, and she basked in the attention he gave her, but he stopped all too abruptly.

"I'll get the baby, you get dressed," he said. "The
pancakes are getting cold. And I'm starved."

He delivered a pat to her bottom, not unlike the
one he'd given his nephew. Discipline tempered by
love. A glimpse of the father he'd be? *If they were
mine, I would have turned them over my knee.* "Yeah,
right." Hannah smiled to herself.

The pancakes were not cold. They were hot and
Mike's mother kept them coming.

"Coffee, Maudie?" Shamus asked his wife as she
moved from stove to table. He poured a cup, mea-

sured out cream and sugar and took a sip. "Just the way you like it," he said, handing it to his wife along with a peck on the cheek.

FALLON SEEMED CONTENT with the constant attention. So Hannah tried not to mind that she hadn't held her daughter all day. Hannah had found something to wear to the party. Though not as dressy as she would have liked, she wasn't as naked as Mike made her feel every time he looked over with those hungry eyes.

The dinner party was larger than she'd expected, about one hundred guests—friends and family, their parish priest, the ladies club. The open bar and the local oldies band kept the dance floor full. The food was served buffet style and the lack of assigned tables encouraged guests to move about freely.

"What is it you do exactly, Hannah?" one of Mike's sister's was asking her. "None of this Navy SEAL business like my brother, I hope?"

"I fly helicopters."

"Sounds dangerous. I think I'll stick to raising my brood. That's about all the adventure I need."

"You moved from Colorado, dear?" Maude asked, dipping a shrimp into the cocktail sauce.

"Temporarily. I sold my condo before moving out here because I knew I'd be upgrading to a house with a yard for Fallon when we went back."

"You're not staying in California, then? I thought Michael said you'd bought a house in Coronado?"

"As an investment. My stock portfolio has been kind of flat lately. I wanted to take some of the money out and put it in real estate. But I have a job waiting for me at Hall-Petrone."

Her plans to move back were based on sound economics. She'd still have to make a living when this was all over.

Would Mike have a reason to travel to Colorado? Either way they'd likely only see him a couple of times a year. He'd be deployed the rest of the time.

"Where have I heard that name Hall-Petrone?"

"They've been in the papers lately. Next week my boss, Peter Petrone, will ring the bell at the New York Stock Exchange to celebrate going public."

"How exciting. Now is this a good stock tip? Because I belong to a ladies investment group through my church. We're mostly a social club you understand. But we each put in twenty-five dollars a month."

"Those clubs usually do very well because of the diversity. It's a good investment. I negotiated a stock option clause into my contract with the company two years ago, just waiting for this day."

"Now this wouldn't be considered insider trading, would it?" Maude whispered.

"SHE IS SO OUT OF YOUR LEAGUE," Meg reached for her beer, "Gucci luggage? Prada handbag and shoes? DKNY slacks and blouse? I bet you don't even know the labels."

"Never heard of them," Mike admitted.

"She's giving investment advice tonight. You might want to listen in."

"I have ears. There's more than one way to make money. One way is to save it. Not handing it over to your sister is another."

"Thanks for the check, by the way. It'll be worth it when you see the look on their faces." Meg leaned a hip against the bandstand where he'd planted his butt after the band had taken a break. "So back to your girlfriend."

"She's not my girlfriend. She's Fallon's mother."

"Whatever she is, I like her. A little uptight. But you two could be good for each other. Think she'd let me do a feature?"

"You'll have to ask her." Mike's eyes strayed to Hannah as she approached.

"We were just talking about you," Meg said. "I don't know if Mike told you, I'm a photo journalist who sometimes gets stuck writing features for the only rag in town. What would you say to an interview? My big brother here has never consented to so much as a quote about his Navy SEALs."

"I'd be flattered," Hannah agreed.

"I'm interested in the single mother angle. Is it true that because of the hardship, single parents only make up about seven percent of the military population? I looked up the stats online. Of course, you two do know that roughly forty-one percent of women in the military marry a guy in uniform, right?"

"Didn't know that," Hannah admitted.

"Considering only forty-three percent marry, odds are, Hannah, you're going to end up with a guy about six-two—" she raised her hand to her brother's height "—brown hair, hazel eyes, looks good in a uniform." Meg hid a knowing smile behind her beer. "Want to know how many children you'll have?" She held up two fingers as she took a drink.

"That's enough," Mike said, embarrassed by his sister's stats, and yet at the same time encouraged by them. Hannah's thoughts on the subject were hard to gauge.

"Only six percent of men in the military marry a woman in uniform." Hannah threw the information out like a challenge.

"Only five percent of Seahawk pilots are women," he countered. No matter what the odds, there was always a chance.

"Okay, then," Meg said, cutting through the tension. "We'll squeeze out some time this weekend for that interview. Then next week, or whenever it's convenient, I can drive down to San Diego for a ride in your helicopter and a photo shoot. Sound good? Isn't Spencer Holden with your squadron? I heard he was injured in a crash recently. How's he doing?"

"He's still in the hospital in Manila," Hannah said soberly. "But he's expected to make a full recovery."

"Except for his face, you mean. I'd kill to get to get that first picture—from Hollywood hottie to Scarface," Meg wrote across the air.

Hannah paled. "Excuse me," she said, stepping away from them.

"What did I say?"

"Is there any delay between your brain and your mouth?" Mike asked. "You don't always have to say the first damn thing to pop into your head!"

The wait staff came around with trays of champagne flutes, signaling that it was time for the toast.

Mike hopped up to the stage. Tapping his spoon to his glass to get the party's attention, he called his parents up front.

"A toast," he said, raising his glass. "To Mom and Dad, on their thirty-sixth wedding anniversary. We don't know how they managed to make it this far, but we'd like to think they have another thirty-six ahead. To start them off on that second leg we thought it might be nice if they got the chance to see some of what they missed during all those years of sacrifice while raising a brood to adulthood. We always had a roof overhead, albeit an overcrowded and occasionally leaky one, but there was always plenty of love and food on the table."

"Hear, hear," everyone agreed, even some of his nieces and nephews who were running around with grape juice. Fallon spoke up with a timely squeal that made everyone laugh, and Mike felt a surge of pride hit him.

Then Buddy took center stage and brought on more laughter. "To Mom and Dad—" he raised his glass "—hear, hear."

"Meg." Mike turned the floor over to his youngest sister.

Without further fanfare she handed an envelope to her mother. "We all pitched in to send you on a twenty-day Orient Adventure Cruise, from the South China Sea to the Great Barrier Reef. Start packing because you're leaving for Hong Kong in a few days. From there it's on to Taiwan, Japan, Guam, New Guinea and Australia."

"Oh, my." Their mom put her hand to her breast.

"And you don't have to worry about anything while you're away," Meg added. "We have a schedule all worked out. And Buddy's going to be spending time with each of us."

Tears streamed from his mother's eyes. "I only wear makeup once a year and I know I'm running my mascara. I hope I remembered the waterproof kind this time." She hugged Mike first because he was close, but then surprised him by not continuing around the room. "I have something I'd like to say," she continued.

"It beats all those road trips to Yosemite?" Marla asked.

Mike joined his siblings in laughing and groaning in remembrance of their single family vacation destination.

"Oh," his mother said, "those trips hold some of the best memories of my life. But that's really not what I have to say." She grew serious all of a sudden, too serious, and Mike found himself bracing for an announcement, his mind going over myriad health issues that might arise at his parents' age. "Your father and I have been living a lie…."

A collective gasp.

Mike had a sinking feeling in his gut. If his parents were about to announce their separation, he sure hadn't seen it coming. Sure, their marriage wasn't perfect, and it was a bit old-fashioned by today's standards, but he'd always thought it was solid. Had his mother gotten tired of her role? He turned a scowl on his father. Because if his parents couldn't make it last, no one could.

"Woman, leave it be," his father protested.

"I can't," she said. "I'm sorry, but this needs to be said to all concerned. This is not our thirty-sixth wedding anniversary. It's our thirty-fifth. Mike was a seven-month-baby when we got married. I'm an old woman now and I like the relief of getting that off my chest. Now I've said my piece, but that doesn't mean I'll be giving back this once-in-a-lifetime cruise."

"Well." Mary Margaret broke the ice. "I don't know about anyone else, but I'm ready for dessert."

THE FLOOR DIDN'T OFFER Mike any comfort from his thoughts tonight. Hannah had been quiet the rest of the evening and shunned his advances once they were alone in the room. The crash, Holden, it had been just a few days ago in a whole other world and the event was probably still sinking in. He'd tried to talk to her about it, but she'd shut down on him.

Fallon stirred, then whimpered.

He was up in a heartbeat and standing over her.

Changing his daughter's soggy diaper, he comforted her with soft-spoken words, then carried her out the door while Hannah continued to sleep.

"I suppose you're hungry," he whispered when he reached the hall.

In answer to his question, she latched on to his bottom lip with her chubby fist. Together they made a buh-buh-buh sound. "Can you say, 'da-da'?" He tried to coach her into trying out the new syllable, but she wasn't having any of it. "Da-da?" he repeated, following the soft glow of night-lights to the kitchen. His daughter rewarded his efforts with a bright smile.

Mike snagged a premade bottle from the refrigerator. While that heated, he poured himself a bowl of cereal. The idea of interacting with this tiny human being he'd created still seemed impossible to him.

They settled on the couch in the living room. He turned the TV on, keeping the volume low. They ate by the soft glow, but he spent more time watching his daughter than the tube. He loved the way she kept her eyes focused on his face, even as she sucked.

His parents' marriage had started with little more than this. Maybe he and Hannah had a chance. Fallon was worth the effort. What would it take to convince Hannah?

Taping his sister's mouth shut might be a start.

HANNAH'S INTERNAL body clock went off some time after 0400. When she woke to total silence and an empty crib, cries of alarm went off in her head. She craned her neck to get a look over the opposite side of the bed, but McCaffrey was gone, too.

Logic told her he had the baby. But that didn't stop her need to make sure her daughter was being cared for.

She threw back the covers and grabbed one of Mike's discarded shirts, which she threw on over her pajamas.

On the landing, she paused.

Fallon and Mike were in the living room. Fallon rested against Mike's shoulder, and he was patting her back. "On the count of three," he said. "One, two…" Father and daughter belched in sync. "Good girl!"

The baby obviously thought he was some kind of belching god. Her little movements became animated, and she laughed out loud.

"Should we do it again?" he asked Fallon.

"I would have fed her." Hannah took those last few steps. "You should have woken me up." It came out sounding like an accusation.

Mike looked up self-consciously. "The baby and I wanted some chow. Thought you could use the rest."

He handed Fallon over, then tucked his hands in his armpits as if he didn't quite know what to do with them now that they were empty.

For some reason it irritated Hannah to realize Fallon had been spending quality time with her father.

What was the point of all this holding and changing and feeding? Did he feel duty-bound? Hannah had no reason to believe that McCaffrey's sudden interest in parenting was anything more than a passing fad.

The first time he was away for six, or more, months at a time, he'd come back a stranger. And when the novelty wore off, he'd start to find other things to do with the time he was home.

Fallon would suffer for the prolonged estrangement. Not Mac. And Hannah'd be damned if that would happen. There would be no butterfly kisses and absolutely no belching on her watch. He made early-morning feedings into playtime, while she was lucky to stay awake through those few precious moments.

What about her quality time with her baby?

She stifled a yawn while McCaffrey looked ready to take on the day. "Coffee?" he asked.

The aroma was already coming from the kitchen. She nodded only because she knew she wouldn't be going back to bed anytime soon.

Fallon reached for Mike as Hannah followed him into the kitchen. The awful truth was, she was jealous of her baby's father. Fallon smiled more for him, laughed out loud for him, and Hannah didn't even know if she'd ever done that before. One of many firsts she'd missed out on.

It was all fine and good that he could get up and

play with the baby, then just hand her back. In the end Hannah would be the one left holding their daughter.

He poured her a cup and took his usual sip. It was just too much for her.

"Stop doing that!"

"What?" He looked confused, leaning back against the counter to sulk into his own cup.

Hannah sat down at the table, trying to regain control of a restless baby and her own jealousy and resentment.

McCaffrey set his cup on the countertop behind him. "Want me to take her?" He held out his arms.

Fallon almost dived for him. "I've got her," Hannah snapped, fumbling to get a better hold on her bundle.

Mike frowned. Hannah scowled, and Fallon cried despite Hannah's best efforts to coddle her.

"Good morning," Maude said, tying her robe as she stepped into the kitchen.

"I'm sorry. I hope we didn't wake you." Hannah remembered her manners and apologized.

Maude shrugged it off. "I'm always awake this early. Who do you think set the coffee timer for five o'clock? Why don't you go catch up on your sleep, Hannah. I know I never got enough as a new mother. Mike and I've got the baby," she said, neatly extracting Fallon from Hannah's arms.

Hannah had been outmaneuvered by a pro. Hannah had the feeling Mrs. M. had heard much of their conversation and had guessed at the source of Hannah's motives and irritability. She'd been given no choice but to be rude to Mike's mother or retreat.

McCaffrey entered the bedroom a few minutes later without their daughter. Hannah was in the bathroom with the door open. She put her toothbrush away and wiped the back of her hand across her mouth. Catching a glimpse of him in the mirror, she hesitated before drying her hands on the hanging towel.

She turned out the bathroom light and stepped into the bedroom all without saying a word. Moving to her suitcase, she put away her toiletries.

And that's when he finally realized she was packing. "What's up," he asked.

She turned to face him. "What's the point to all this, Mike? I'm tired of acting the part of the happy family. And quite frankly, I can't see you as a father." In truth, the glimpse she'd gotten scared her. All her old insecurities surfaced in that instant. "Even if I'd had the chance to tell you about Fallon, you would have missed her birth. How many birthdays and milestones are you going to miss?"

"Don't do this," he pleaded. "Don't make me choose between duty and my daughter."

"Dammit, McCaffrey! I'm not asking you to choose. I'm asking you to let us go. Fallon's just a baby. You might miss an occasional birthday, but she's going to spend her life missing you." She could see she was tearing out his heart. She was tearing out her own. She turned back to the suitcase and zipped closed the lid with a finality that ripped through the room. "I can't do this. I'm not strong enough to do this. I want to go home."

CHAPTER SEVENTEEN

NAVAL AMPHIBIOUS BASE
Coronado, California

MIKE TOWELED OFF, then tossed his towel to the bench in the Team's locker room. He stood naked in front of his open locker. His Chase-Durer waited for him on the top shelf, along with the rest of his personal effects, and he felt the overwhelming desire to see a gold band beside it.

He brushed the inscription with his thumb before strapping the watch on. What would that be like, piecing himself back together after a mission, knowing he had a wife and daughter waiting for him at home?

He'd always been a little bit afraid to want that.

Now that he had a daughter he was afraid the reality wasn't as simple as what he might have wanted it to be. Hannah didn't need him and she didn't want him. She'd made that clear the other morning when they'd wound up leaving the farm a day early.

He didn't know what Hannah wanted.

Hannah didn't know what Hannah wanted. And that was the real problem. She'd said she needed time and space—away from him. So he'd left her, and his daughter, alone all week, hoping Hannah would be able to figure out exactly what she should do.

He'd kept himself busy during the day. At night he rotated through the take-out menus on his refrigerator.

He thought maybe what she really wanted was to stay home with the baby. She could do that and still be in uniform with just one phone call to Petrone.

Where would that leave him?

Separated from his daughter by fifteen hundred miles. But Hannah would have what she wanted. His daughter would have what she needed—her mother. And Petrone would have everything Mike could ever hope to have.

Mike picked up his cell phone and hit the speed dial, filtering out the sounds of the locker room.

"Hall-Petrone Aerospace Tech," a woman answered.

"I'd like to speak with Peter Petrone."

"May I ask who's calling, please?"

"McCaffrey. Tell him it's Commander Mike McCaffrey, and I have a favor to ask…"

"Hold one moment, please."

He wrapped the towel back around his waist and switched ears as easy-listening music began to play in the background.

A guy Mike recognized from the Leap Frogs, the Navy SEALs parachute jumping team, walked in calling his name. "Commander McCaffrey?"

"Yo." Mike waved him over while he was still waiting for Petrone.

The guy stepped up to him. "Sir, is your full name Sean Michael McCaffrey?"

"Yes," Mike said with a touch more caution. He lowered the phone from his ear, just now realizing this Frog moonlighted as a process server because his day job gave him access to the Naval base and its personnel.

"Sorry, Commander. Consider yourself served." All conversation around them ceased as the guy slapped legal papers into Mike's palm.

NAVAL AIR STATION NORTH ISLAND
Coronado, California

"SORRY, MA'AM," her yeoman apologized from the door as McCaffrey pushed his way into her office.

Hannah stood. "It's all right. Just go ahead and close the door behind the commander."

McCaffrey took the court order in his back pocket and tossed it to the desk. "One weekend a month, two weeks a year? Sounds like reserve duty to me. I'm an active duty dad. Nothing less than joint custody, Han!"

Crossing her arms, she took a deep breath. It wasn't as if she wasn't expecting this. "You'll be lucky if you can find one weekend a month and two weeks in the summer to spend with your daughter. I have no objection to Fallon spending that time with your family when you're not available, but I'd like your parenting plan as soon as possible. This isn't easy for me, either, Mike. She's just a baby—"

"And you have so much more time to spend with her than I do."

"That's not fair."

"This—" he stabbed his finger to the document "—isn't fair. I stopped by legal on the way over. They said one-sixth of my base pay per child." He reached into his back pocket again and this time pulled out his checkbook. He ripped off the top check and handed it to her. "Six months back child support. I'll arrange to have monthly payments deposited to your account—"

"It's not about the money, Mike. I don't even *need* your money... Thank you," she apologized, realizing it wasn't about the money for him, either. She caught a glimpse of the check design. Smiling at his neat signature and the whimsy that made him pick Snoopy the Flying Ace, she relented. "What do you propose we do, Mike?"

He removed his ball cap, combed steady fingers through his hair, then stood on the opposite side of her desk with his legs spread and his arms folded. "Move in together," he said, looking her square in the eye.

She must have stared for a full minute, trying to figure out the meaning behind his words. "Marriage isn't the answer."

"I didn't ask you to marry me," he countered. "Or to sleep with me."

Embarrassed by her own presumption, she felt

heat creep up her neck. "There are only four bed-rooms. And I was going to make one over into Fal-lon's nursery."

"We kick your mother out. I plan to keep my place, and she can stay there for as long as our little arrangement continues."

"And what about Sammy? Are we going to kick her out, too?"

"I think we both know that as duel military par-ents, we need your sister. You may not get more time with Fallon if I move in, but with both of us sharing full responsibility you'll get more quality time with her."

"It'll never work."

"It's going to work because it's the grown-up thing to do. We can split our kid. Or we can split our time. The way I see it neither of those two options is really ideal. So we combine forces as one family unit."

"You make it sound so simple, yet I know this is going to be complicated."

"Is that a maybe?"

She caught the twitch at the corner of his mouth and smiled. Still she hedged.

"I can't be your roommate, Mike. I mean it's not realistic to think that we could just live together, and not *live* together. It would be like kids playing house where everything is just pretend. Real people have real relationships, real feelings and real fights." Her hand gestures became animated. "I fight with my mother and sister all the time, but I still love them and forgive them. What would we be basing this relationship on?" She held her palms up, waiting for his answer.

He perched on her desk. "Okay, if you insist I'll sleep with you."

EARLY SATURDAY MORNING McCaffrey showed up at the house just as Hannah returned from taking Fallon for a ride in her new baby jogger. She unlocked the door and there he was sauntering up her walkway.

His visit wasn't all that unexpected. What *was* unexpected was the brand spanking new Jeep Cherokee parked at her curb. A Ford Bronco and an eighteen-wheeler pulled up behind the Jeep.

"Come in," she invited, leaving the door open. "What's with the new SUV?"

"No kid of mine is riding in a vehicle with a roll bar. Samantha—" he tossed her sister a set of keys as soon as he stepped in the door "—title's in the glove box. The old Jeep is yours. Catch a ride with Itch and pick it up. Go have some fun. Stay out as late as you want tonight."

McCaffrey was really moving in!

Mac, two of his brothers-in-law, Itch and Buddy were moving things in and out of *her* house. Her mother's things were loaded onto the eighteen-wheeler while Mac's stuff was unloaded in their place, though he didn't have as much as her mother.

Hannah's furniture, which had been stuffed into her bedroom and the nursery, was brought out. All she had to do was carry Fallon around on her hip and point and someone put things where she wanted them. Her bed was assembled. She could actually move around in her bedroom. The nursery was completely emptied and readied for the paint she'd purchased earlier that week.

Okay, there were some benefits to having a man around. Mike had kicked her mother out and in such a way that her mother was agreeable to it!

"That's everything," McCaffrey announced, after he and Itch hauled his mattress and box spring to her mother's old room.

She stood in the doorway eyeing him warily as they finished assembling the bed. Itch took his leave and McCaffrey backed her out the door.

"No crossing this threshold." He drew an imaginary line with his toe, then took the baby from her. She'd agreed to let him move in on the condition that their situation stay platonic. She was afraid any other kind of relationship with McCaffrey would spell disaster for their daughter. They were as separate as the oil in her Seahawk and the water Navy SEALs thrived in.

The house had grown quiet now that the three of them were alone and she stated her doubts out loud. "This isn't going to work."

"What's not going to work? If you're right about me being good at leaving and staying away, then you'll hardly notice I'm here. I'll just be the guy who writes a check once a month."

"We'll see, won't we?"

"What do you say we go pick out some baby furniture."

There was something backward about his logic, but she'd been too shocked to figure it out.

"Almost forgot—" He picked up an envelope from his dresser. "You might want to put this in a safe place. It's my new will. Death benefits and everything goes to Fallon, except provisions for Buddy and a flame-out party for the guys. There's a letter to Fallon, too—just in case. Thought I'd add a few pages every year."

"This whole conversation is making me uncomfortable."

"Then you're really going to hate that there's a letter for you, too."

"I don't want it." She pushed his hand away. "Just put it all somewhere safe."

"Accepting this letter doesn't mean I'm going to die. It just means I'm putting my affairs in order. We should talk about that—"

"My affairs are in order—"

"I don't want to leave anything unsaid. It'll be here, on my dresser when you're ready to accept it."

Her throat burned. "I won't *ever* accept it."

MIKE DIDN'T PUSH the letter issue. Furniture shopping took less than an hour because she agreed to the set he'd already picked out. When they got home, Hannah started painting while he assembled the crib in her bedroom. They'd wait until the fumes died to move the baby into the nursery.

Fallon sat in her bouncy chair, content to watch him with the screwdriver and giving a giggle whenever he cursed at the instructions. He'd have to learn to watch his language around her or she'd soon have the vocabulary of a sailor.

He actually said "sugar" when he stabbed himself with the screwdriver once again.

He'd thought about asking his mother for the family crib, but realized it belonged in the house where he grew up to be used by a whole new generation of visitors. Besides there was nothing wrong with starting his own tradition. The crib he'd picked out came in a light finish with matching dresser and changing table.

The doorbell rang. "I'll get it!" He shoved the screwdriver back into his tool belt, which he wasn't wearing, and pushed the baby into the hall where Hannah could keep an eye on her.

He paid for the pizza, grabbed a bottle for the baby and a couple of beers and headed back up the stairs. "Break time. Hey, this looks nice," he said, taking in the half white, half shocking-pink walls and the sherbet rainbow border.

"I'll leave the windows open tonight. Maybe we'll be able to move her things in after the weekend." When she didn't say anything about being in a hurry to move the baby out of her room, he smiled to himself. He'd left her and the baby alone enough this week, and he didn't intend to leave them alone anymore.

They picnicked out in the hall on the hardwood floor. A breeze from the nursery carried whiffs of paint and pine. To Mike it smelled like a fresh start.

Hannah pushed to her feet. "I'm going to clean up the mess in the nursery and take this box to the trash."

"I need a shower, then I'll give this little lady her bath. Just point me in the right direction."

"You can use the master bath," Hannah offered. "There should be clean towels and the baby's things are all in there. Are you sure you don't want me to bathe her?"

"Nope. I've got it covered."

They went their separate ways. Sometime later he emerged from the bathroom—soaked, shirtless and barefoot. But the baby was clean and dry. Cleaning up the bathroom afterward though had taken him quite a while so he was surprised that Hannah hadn't been right there knocking on the door.

She wasn't in her bedroom. *Or his.* The painting supplies in the nursery had been cleaned up. "Should we go find momma? And see if she wants to take her turn?"

"Buh-buh. Buh-buh," Fallon answered.

"Da-da," he started their favorite game again.

The living room was dark, except for what he

thought was the TV. Until he discovered an 8-mm movie being projected onto a screen.

"I found the whole box in the trash," she said, without looking up. But it was pretty obvious by her sniffles that she'd been crying.

He was going to kill Rosemary. What was the woman thinking? He picked up a couple of the empty metal containers and read the hand-printed labels. Hannah's sixth birthday. Summer BBQs. Fourth-of-July picnic. Didn't Rosemary realize Hannah and Samantha would cherish these memories of their father?

He watched the grainy image of a little girl blowing out six candles on a cake. It wasn't hard to tell which of the buzz-cut military men in the background was her father. He was the guy doting on her.

The movie went white after a couple more frames. Then the film started flapping around in the projector.

"How many times have you watched this?" he asked, noting the reels were only about fifteen minutes long.

"Three."

"That's enough for tonight then." He helped her to her feet and turned off the projector. "To bed."

"But Sammy isn't home yet." She gave the feeble protest, even though she was already letting him lead the way upstairs.

"She's over twenty-one and has her own key."

While still holding Fallon, he showed Hannah to the bathroom where he had about one hundred candles burning, or at least it had seemed that way when he'd been lighting each one. The steamy bathroom and hot bath had been his stage for a seduction that wasn't going to take place now.

She was still moving like a zombie and didn't even close the door when she stripped. So he played the part of the gentleman, turning his back to make up the crib and lay their daughter down in it.

He brushed Fallon's hair back. "Don't sweat it, sweet pea. Daddy doesn't make a move without a plan and a backup. This one has three phases. Co-parenting, co-habitation and co-dependency. We're working up to commitment. SEALs and Seahawks have a symbiotic relationship—they need each other. But right now, Daddy has to see about a little damage control."

He left Fallon in the crib. Downstairs, he locked up the house, leaving the porch light on for Samantha. Then he packed up the movies and projector. There were slides and photographs in the box, as well.

He poured Hannah a glass of white wine from a bottle in the refrigerator. Then he hauled the whole mess upstairs just as she was coming out of the bathroom in her robe. Her eyes were still puffy from crying.

"Where would you like me to put this?" he asked.

"The window seat is fine for now." He set it down and brought her the glass of wine. She clutched at the tie ends of her robe. "The bath, the candles, the wine."

She took the glass from his hand. "I thought we agreed to keep our relationship on neutral ground."

"Nothing less than total surrender, Han. But we'll save it for later."

HANNAH HAD STAYED UP late looking through old photos and had planned to sleep in the next morning. There was the rescheduled HCS-9 and ST-11 picnic that afternoon and she wanted to rest up for the tug-of-war, at least that was her excuse, but Sammy walked in carrying a breakfast tray. "Rise and shine!"

"You're up awfully early after staying out so late," Hannah said, sitting up in bed and eyeing her sister suspiciously. "What's this?"

"Happy birthday."

"You know I don't like the fuss."

"No fuss, it's French toast," she said, lifting the lid. "And I got you a present." Sammy handed over the shoe box and Hannah opened the lid on a pair of white heels with a satin finish.

"They're from my hope chest, four-hundred-dollar Manolo Blahniks," Sammy said. "You can consider them something borrowed, or something old since I've had them forever and it looks like you're going to be walking down the aisle first."

"Sam—" Hannah started to protest.

But then Fallon began to fuss, and Sammy lifted her out of the crib. "Are you singing 'Happy Birthday' to Mommy? I'll get her diaper changed, then bring her bottle and cereal right up. Then maybe we could sort through some of those old photos Mac was telling me about."

"Mornin', birthday girl," McCaffrey said, propping up the doorjamb with her morning cup of coffee in his hand.

To quote McCaffrey, today was a pretty damn good day. No bullets.

WHILE HANNAH TOOK Fallon out in the baby jogger, Mike picked up the phone and called Rosemary Stanton.

"Hello?"

"It's Mike, do you have a minute?" He got straight to the point. "Hannah found some memorabilia of her father in the trash yesterday. She was very upset by it. I think you owe her an apology. At the very least an explanation."

"You mean his collection of old comic books and baseball cards?"

"No, I mean the box of photographs."

"I told Buddy to carry that box out to the moving van. And that he could have the box of Van's old comic books and baseball cards if he wanted them or take them out to the trash. Oh, my," she said, realizing what must have happened. "Was she very upset?"

"I think she'll be relieved to hear you didn't throw them away. I apologize for Buddy's misunderstanding. You should also know those comic books and baseball cards you gave him are probably worth something. I'll see that he returns them—"

"Nonsense. I know how much they're worth, but I could no more bear to sell them than I could to look at them. Let Buddy keep whatever enjoyment or money he gets from them."

"Thank you. In the future though, if you find any more of your deceased husband's belongings could you tell me first before giving or throwing them away? It might be something Hannah or Samantha or even Fallon would like to keep. And we'll wait and see what they decide about the comic books and baseball cards before I take it up with Buddy."

"Whatever you think is best," she agreed.

"We'll see you at dinner tonight. I thought I'd take Hannah and Fallon on a little outing today…" He filled Rosemary in on the rest of his plan.

CABRILLO MONUMENT PARK
Point Loma, California

"SIX DAYS. SIX NIGHTS. You owe me a kayaking trip," McCaffrey bragged as he pulled his Jeep Cherokee out of the parking lot of the Old Point Loma Lighthouse on the way home from Cabrillo Monument Park and the HCS-9/ST-11 picnic.

Hannah still wore the mud that proved her Wings had lost the tug-of-war to his Warriors, so she'd insisted on sitting on a towel to protect the upholstery.

This was their first family "outing" and no one from either unit seemed surprised when they'd shown up together with the baby. No apologies. No excuses. McCaffrey had made it clear that her daughter was his.

Exhausted, Hannah relaxed against the seat for the ride home. The peninsula jutted into San Diego Bay. Known for its secluded coves and staggering cliffs, the spectacular view of the city and ocean alone were worth the trip.

"Is this the right road home?" she asked as they followed the signs to Fort Rosecrans Military Reservation. Hannah shifted uncomfortably in her seat. That was where her father was buried. She reached back to the car seat and brushed her daughter's hair.

"We'll get there soon. You want to get out and take a look around?"

"Not really."

"I'd like to stop and pay respects to a couple of my men, if you don't mind."

How could she object? She knew ST-11 had suffered causalities just before she'd taken command of HCS-9. So she didn't say anything. But she didn't expect him to open up the back door and unstrap Fallon from her seat.

"You coming?" he asked.

The rows of dignified markers ended with fresh graves awaiting headstones. Compelled by something—she wasn't exactly sure what—Hannah stepped out of the Jeep and followed McCaffrey.

He jostled Fallon to keep her contented and pointed out the numbered graves where his men were buried. "Chief Paul Zahn. His sister was a rescue swimmer attached to your squadron. I think Bell took her place. She took it pretty hard when she pulled his body out of the water, but I spoke to her a couple days ago and she's doing okay. Calhoun was one of my lieutenants. He left behind a widowed bride. Hadn't even been married a full year, and we were gone most of that time."

"That's so sad for his bride."

"She's doing okay, too. Life goes on."

He pointed to an empty grave. "Normally, the military doesn't skip over grave sites—the bodies are planted in numbered order. But this one was supposed to be for Nash's wife. The family put up a fuss so she wasn't buried here, but under normal circumstances military personnel can choose to be buried with their spouse. One on top of the other."

Now that he'd pointed it out, she noticed a couple of headstones with two names. And a couple of other grave sites that had been skipped over.

"Those are for military couples," he said. "A military couple can be buried together or side by side. I want that choice, Han, whether I'm that next one, or buried off somewhere in the distance. I want to spend eternity, and whatever time I have left on this earth, with you." He stood there, holding their future, looking at her. "I don't know how to say it any plainer than that."

"Are you proposing to me in a cemetery?"

"I'm proposing," he said, drawing her near, "that we take that walk over to your father's grave."

The first steps were the easiest because she

hadn't noticed McCaffrey had been dragging him with her all along. But with the last few steps came the painful memories of her father's flag-draped coffin and a little girl hiding under a table with her baby sister.

"Happy birthday to me," she whispered, her voice cracking. "They should have buried you on a different day. Oh, God, I've hated her for that…for packing. They put you in a box, and she put everything else in there right along with you. You're not off the hook, either. I'm still mad at you for not coming home when you were supposed to. It's been twenty-seven years and I still miss you, Daddy."

McCaffrey pulled her to him. She sobbed into his chest, holding on to him and Fallon, until finally years of untapped memories returned. Sad, bitter-sweet, joyful memories.

Fallon started to wail. Hannah lifted her tear-stained face to give her daughter a radiant smile. "Come here," she said with outstretched arms and McCaffrey transferred their daughter into them. "This is just where your grandpa stands watch over the base," she said, taking in the panoramic view of the Naval Amphibious Base. "And down there, that's where your daddy works. Promise me," she said to McCaffrey, "she'll always be a part of your life, and I promise you no matter what, I'll never let her forget."

"Make me the same promise," he said against her lips.

CHAPTER EIGHTEEN

"I'LL GET IT," Sammy said when the doorbell rang that evening. All four of them were in the kitchen where she'd been helping Mike prepare dinner.

Mike was much more comfortable sharing a house than he'd thought he would be. Of course, this was only day two, the novelty of living with two women and a baby hadn't worn off yet. He had to make sure it never did.

He removed his apron. "Now would probably be a good time to warn you—" he leaned in to whisper in Hannah's ear "—you have carrot on your cheek." He licked it away. "Yum," he said for his daughter's benefit. "Just as good as a lactate rigger."

"That's warrior Gatorade for the uninitiated," Hannah said to Fallon. Lactate riggers are Kool-Aid packets dumped into a bag of IV solution. "They taste yucky, carrots taste yummy." Fallon giggled and Hannah continued the baby talk. "Sometimes when Daddy's in the desert all he has left to drink are his medical supplies. Isn't he a silly man?"

"Isn't he a 'resourceful' man? is what you should

be teaching her. Right, sweet pea?" he called on his daughter for backup. "Oh, as I was saying before I got distracted by licking you, I invited a few people over for your birthday dinner."

"You what?" She paused with a spoonful of orange baby mash just out of Fallon's reach. In her high chair, the baby stretched forward as far as she could. When that didn't work she batted at the spoon. Mashed carrots went flying.

"Hannah, Mike," Captain Loring greeted them from the doorway, then set a present down on the table.

"Hannah, you're supposed to feed the baby those carrots, not wear them," Rosemary said. "Is that her first solid food? How could you let me miss it?"

MCCAFFREY THOUGHT he was being clever, inviting the captain to dinner. So he could what? Give her the sugarcoated version of how her father had died—that would be about as palatable as a lactate rigger.

The doorbell rang again. "I'll get it." Hannah excused herself while her mother took over feeding the baby. She'd been expecting her mother, and not all that surprised to see the captain with her, but when she opened the door to find Webb, Boomer, his foot still in a cast, and Spence standing there, she launched herself into her co-pilot's arms and kissed him full on the lips. His face was still swollen, and he still had stitches, but to her he looked better than good. "When did they release you from the hospital?"

"I got back Friday."

"Why weren't you at the picnic?" She looked to Webb and Boomer, who had been there and hadn't said anything, before ushering them all inside. Coming up the walk behind them was Russell Parish, his arm still in a sling, and his crew, Hunter, Kia Makani and Quinn—all carrying presents. "Come in, everybody," she said, but before she could even close the door, the Bells—the admiral, Lu and Libby—along with Mike's XO and the rest of his squad arrived.

When she finally shut the door it was to find her mother holding a cake with seven candles on it. McCaffrey was setting up the projector and screen she'd discovered in the trash the other night. It took a full minute for her to realize that everyone carried gifts and wore retro clothes.

This was some sort of reenactment of the birthday she'd missed. Her eyes locked on Mike and she mouthed the words *thank you.*

"HANNAH, I'M SO SORRY," her mother said later as they were clearing dishes. "Michael told me how upset you were when you found those pictures in the trash."

"Mike explained everything to me, Mother. It's all right. Buddy didn't know better. He thought he was doing just as he was told, I'm sure."

"That's not why I'm apologizing, Hannah. I let my pain rob you of so many things. I couldn't even look at those old photographs, but I should have realized you girls needed to. Sammy was just so little. And you…you were always so strong. Back then it was all I could do to keep myself and my family together. I was young, money was tight…. The apartments kept getting smaller—"

"I know, Mom." Hannah pulled her mother close.

"Oh, look at me, I'm a mess. I need a tissue. In my purse." She waved Hannah toward her handbag, hanging on a kitchen chair while she composed herself.

"I always thought I'd inherited my strength from him. But I can see I inherited a little from both of you. You did good, Mom," she said, wanting to reassure her mother. "I'm healthy, and I'm happy. And only a little messed up in the man department." But McCaffrey was working on that.

She decided to change the subject. "So are you and the captain…" She raised an eyebrow.

"Oh, Hannah, the things you say. I'm pretty sure I heard Fallon say, 'shit' today. How are we supposed to write that in her baby book?"

"She's only five months old, Mother. She says, buh-buh. And that's for her bottle *and* her daddy."

"Well, I'm pretty sure I'm not doing *anything* because I don't even remember how—"

"Then you'll just have to let the captain take point on this one. Trust me, Mom, he may be a widower, but I'm pretty sure he remembers how that op goes down."

"Sammy sent me in for another piece of cake," Loring announced his presence.

Her mother blushed. "I'll cut it."

Hannah snickered, but kept rinsing and loading the dishwasher. "How's retired life treating you, Captain?" she asked to ease the tension in the room.

But it did nothing to ease the ache she felt for McCaffrey a while later when they'd finally said goodnight to all their guests. Would she have to get out the signal flags and direct him to her bedroom, or did he already know there were no separate beds tonight?

"You didn't open my present," he said as he closed the door one final time. Everyone had given her memorabilia of some kind. A framed picture of the admiral and her father. One with her father and Captain Loring. Her mother had given her his letter jacket from the University of Wisconsin, Oshkosh. Her sister had put together a scrapbook. Her crew and Mac's squad had all brought little mementos that had to do with her own career.

What more could she possibly need? "I thought this party was your present."

He handed her a file folder. "Freedom of information act. His file has been declassified for years. He died in a failed rescue attempt of POWs. The helicopter went down under enemy fire in the Mekong Delta. And he drowned while saving the life of the pilot—one Jon 'JJ' Loring, the only survivor of the crash. I suspect your mother already knows all that."

Hannah pressed the file to her breast.

"Aren't you going to read it?"

"Later, maybe," she said.

"Here's something else to read in your spare

time." He handed her a copy of the *Odyssey*. Inside it was a sealed letter. "When you're ready," he said.

"Will you tell me what it says? The important parts anyway," she said with a hitch in her voice.

He tugged her toward him by the tail of the shirt that she wore over her tank top. The shirt slipped to reveal her shoulder and he kissed her there. "It says, I want to be there for all the birthdays and mile-stones, even when I'm not." He pushed down the thin strap of her tank top and kissed her throat.

"I want to keep you safe and at home." He trailed kisses along her collarbone as he spoke. "But I won't, because that's not the woman you are. And I don't think it's even possible for me to love another woman. The one woman I want is a lot of things. Some of which are dangerous." He stopped kissing her to look her in the eye. "I'll be selfish and jealous and at times you'll be glad that I'm not around. And when I am, I'll be under foot."

Encouraged by her half smile, he continued. "I want to wake up with you every morning and make love to you every night, but I won't be able to, so every sunset and sunrise I'll be thinking of you—even when I shouldn't." He swallowed the lump in his throat. "I want to give you more children, but it's okay if we decide that's not practical, because when I hold you and Fallon, I have all I need and more than I deserve. Because of that, if my life should be cut short, I have no regrets, Hannah."

"Just remember, I have it in writing," she teased. Then she kissed him. And she wasn't teasing.

NAVAL AMPHIBIOUS BASE
Coronado, California

HANNAH ARRIVED at NAS North Island on Monday to find she'd been summoned to Admiral Bell's office for an early-morning meeting. She entered the building at NAB with only minutes to spare.

Which meant she didn't have time to stop by Mike's office first and collect on their bet—Peter had rung the morning bell at the New York Stock Exchange and shortly afterward announced his fuel-cell contract with the United States Navy, immediately sending Hall-Petrone stock skyrocketing. Mike had some crazy idea that she was part of the deal.

While she was glad she'd had the foresight to negotiate those stock options into her contract two years ago, she hadn't had time to sip mimosas with her mother and sister that morning. And the thrill of making money didn't compare to the thrill of making love with Mike. Only his touch caused that over-the-moon feeling and of course sent her crashing back to earth.

He wanted to get married right away, but she wanted to stay in a holding pattern for now. If this was love, his heart, at least, wasn't going anywhere.

She was, however, surprised to find him in the admiral's office. Both men stood when she entered and exchanged covert glances, but when she tried to make eye contact with Mike, he wouldn't.

Or couldn't.

"Lieutenant Commander Stanton come in,

please. Have a seat," the admiral said in a brisk professional manner. "Let me get straight to the point. Commander McCaffrey has just officially informed me that he's the father of your baby. Congratulations to the both of you. I understand you plan to marry?"

"Maybe," she said, without committing.

McCaffrey's mouth became a thin line.

"Mac feels, strongly, that the two of you should not be in combat situations together."

"Really? Because this is the first I'm hearing about it. Is Mac not capable of speaking for himself?" She directed her question and accompanying glare at McCaffrey.

"I knew you'd react this way."

"Then why didn't you give me the courtesy of having this conversation in private?"

"Hannah." It was the first time the admiral had called her by her first name. "I'm afraid this is my fault." He circled the desk and perched on a corner. "No one is trying to make this decision for you. Mike just came to me to discuss options. I'm the one who pulled you in here."

Hannah clasped her hands in her lap to retain some semblance of control. "And my options are— what? Resign my commission?"

"A reassignment might better serve the needs of the Navy. Hall-Petrone has requested you liaise with his company on several occasions. You could essentially serve out your active duty in your civilian job."

"Move back to Colorado?" Now that McCaffrey wasn't running, was he pushing her away?

"I spoke with Petrone," McCaffrey broke in. "He's willing to consider moving production of the fuel cell to North Island."

So he wasn't pushing her away, just trying to set her on a shelf like a china doll, afraid she'd get broken in a sandbox full of boys and their toys. He'd said he'd want to keep her safe at home, but wouldn't because it wasn't possible for him to love another woman. Ha!

"It's the difference between combat ready and combat support, Han," McCaffrey said. "It's just the way it is. No one here is saying you're not an asset."

No one was saying it. But they were saying she was expendable. Here. At home. No one needed her. A wry smile touched her lip. No one needed her except Peter and Hall-Petrone. But this was her choice. The admiral had said so himself. "And if I don't find either of those choices acceptable?"

An exasperated sigh escaped McCaffrey. He pushed to his feet. With folded arms, he started pacing a hole into the admiral's Oriental rug. "Just say you'll stand down from joint missions. No one's asking you not to fly or even command.

"No? Putting restrictions on my command and flight is asking an awful lot. My country called. I answered." Hannah stood, as well, so everyone in the room wasn't towering over her. "I agreed to take command of HCS-9 for two years and that's what I'm going to do. No restrictions," she said to McCaffrey's back.

He turned to square off with her.

She turned to Admiral Bell. "Correct me if I'm wrong, Admiral, but the Navy actually encourages family members to serve together, including husbands and wives who aren't otherwise in the same chain of command. True?"

"True." The admiral looked at McCaffrey. "I'm going to need an answer now because I have the next assignment for you two. His name is Sebastian," the admiral passed her the folder with photos of the dead Tango she'd shot, paper clipped to the front. "Sebastian Kahn, half Filipino, half Arab bastard son of Mullah Kahn, head of al-Ayman." The admiral emphasized the words by slapping his file and tossing it to the table. "I need you both back in the P.I. ASAP."

Hannah glared at Mac. "My choice is to do the job I was called to do. If we're through, Admiral, I need to ready my men."

Admiral Bell nodded. Hannah left his office with McCaffrey hot on her heels.

"Don't I have some say in this?" he demanded, ushering her by the elbow into his office and closing the door.

"I'm perfectly capable of making my own decisions. My brain. My uterus—" She gave him a visual anatomy lesson. "Which one scares the hell out of you more?"

"Wanting to keep you out of harm's way does not make me some kind of Neanderthal."

"Well, you sure have those fight-or-flight instincts down. But that doesn't mean I'm going to let you drag me around by the hair."

"Those are real bullets flying around out there. Think of our daughter."

"I am thinking of *my* daughter. I think of my daughter every damn day. We're talking about me, Mike. We're talking about you. Your need to control a situation makes you pretty damn good at your job and lousy in relationships. You can't control me. And you certainly can't go around whispering sweet nothings in one ear and orders in the other. Here's your chain of command—" she raised her hand about shoulder level "—and here's mine." She brought her other hand up to the same level. "We are equals. We are peers. The only difference is one of us wears a skirt *sometimes*. You don't get to bring an admiral into the situation to try and manipulate me. You would never do that with one of your male cohorts. Check their wallets. At least half of them are carrying pictures of their babies."

"Are you through yet?"

Her tirade had died, but not her anger. "No, I'm not. This thing between us isn't going to work, Mike. You know it and I know it. But you know what really pisses me off? For two minutes I actually believed in those sweet nothings!"

Both their pagers went off before he could reply.

NAVAL AIR STATION NORTH ISLAND
Coronado, California

THE FIRST AND SECOND waves moved out on time. The third wave developed minor mechanical malfunctions that kept Hannah and McCaffrey pacing the tarmac. SOP required the task force deploy as a unit in case the Team was needed en route. At this point one-third of their unit would be lucky to get there, while two-thirds would be sitting on their hands in the P.I.

Or as McCaffrey put it, "getting all the good action."

"What exactly is the problem?" Hannah asked the pilot of the C-5 that was holding them up.

"We've developed a pretty bad hydraulic fuel leak. Busted hose." He wiped his fuel-covered hands on a rag.

"And let me guess, you don't have any hose on-board? Because of another very recent fuel leak."

The pilot got defensive on his crew's behalf. "Look, my guys have a spotless maintenance record. We called over to supply. You'll just have to sit tight until they get here."

"Not necessarily," Hannah interjected. "Brady," she called the SEAL corpsman over. "Let me see what you have in your medic's kit." She found a piece of tubing about the size she was looking for.

"The pilot of the last C-5 I flew on with a similar problem showed me this trick. If you don't mind flying wheels down?"

The pilot took the hint. "If you can stop the leak, I'll fly her." Which was saying a lot about the man's character and the importance of their mission. A C-5 was a flying warehouse.

Hannah crawled into the wheel well with her crew chief. After being sprayed by hydraulic fluid, they managed to stop the fuel leak. The pilot inspected their repair job and ordered everyone back off the plane while he started up her engines.

Brady passed out sleeping pills for the long flight while the pilot assured himself there were not going to be any fireballs from the spray of fuel.

Hannah refused the sleeping pills. McCaffrey took them. His body, his choice. She knew he ran on adrenaline and testosterone from the minute his pager beeped.

"See you on the flip side," he said as she got ready to board the C-5 and he headed off in the direction of the waiting C-130s. Intel had reported a cargo ship headed toward al-Ayman's island base camp, possibly to off-load munitions.

"Mac!" Itch came running toward them at full speed and handed McCaffrey the box. "You've got a call on the SATCOM. It's the admiral. Urgent."

"McCaffrey." He listened for a moment. "Copy."

He waved his men over. "Listen up," he shouted above the engine noise. "A cruise ship has been hijacked out of Taiwan. We're being rerouted to Guam, then the USS *Enterprise* in the South China Sea. I'll brief you on the plane! Commander, you're going to want to come with me," he said.

Grown men were shoving fingers down their throats like bulimic schoolgirls to get rid of the sleeping pills.

McCaffrey bent over and when he straightened to wipe his mouth, only the flicker in his jaw gave away the fact that his parents were on a cruise ship that had pulled into Taiwan that day.

"Are you okay?" she asked.

But he let her question pass without comment.

Feelings had no place on this op.

"COUGH IT UP," Doc said to Nouri.

"It's not coming," the ensign whined, still trying to force up his sleeping pill.

Mike gathered the rest of his men and Hannah together in the hull of the C-130 for briefing. The noise of the engines and the cold took some getting used to, but at least it kept him awake. At this point he was mainlining caffeine.

"Here's what we know so far." He took out his earplugs for clarity. "The point of origin on the Australian cruise liner, *King Neptune,* was Hong Kong. The *Neptune* pulled into Taiwan at about 0900 their time. Eighty odd international passengers and crew, including at least ten Americans, and we're waiting on an official count for that, remained onboard because of a case of food poisoning or flu—"

"Flu?" Brady asked. "Could we be dealing with the possibility of biological or chemical weapons?"

"That's a strong possibility," Mike answered. "Or intentional poisoning. The hijackers, who originally boarded as wait staff, made their move around noon, catching everyone who'd made it out of their cabins and to the galley, by surprise. They then ordered the captain out to sea. According to our last SitRep the ship was moving south in and out of territorial waters.

"There are only six hijackers on board, so we can assume there may be some passengers still in their rooms. During the initial confusion the captain was able to send out a distress call. But all communication has since ceased."

He sensed Hannah holding her breath. She and Itch were the only ones who knew how very personal this was. He drew comfort just from her being there. Even if he couldn't show it.

"We can assume they're headed to the open waters of the Pacific where they'll be harder to track. If they maintain radio silence we could lose them. A couple of our destroyers and a submarine are trying to intercept before that happens, but their job is to dog tail from the horizon. Our job is to plan and execute a ship takedown. We're it. Bravo Squad and Calypso's three Seahawks. The rest of the task force is to continue on course. I want scenarios. I want schematics. Itch?"

"I'm working on getting us that blueprint, Mac." He continued to hold the open line. SATCOM received pictures via PIRATE technology.

"I want someone on the phone to my sister. She knows this ship's itinerary and possibly has a brochure." He tossed Ajax his picture phone. "It's number five on the speed dial. Get her to send pictures and we'll bootleg to the SATCOM to print them out."

While his men went about following his orders, Mike got up from his squat to stretch. Hannah took a sip from a paper cup and handed it to him.

"Here. It's hot and it's black." She stirred creamer and sugar in her own cup. "They could have gotten off in Taiwan."

He nodded, acknowledging the possibility.

Nouri had fallen asleep in his seat. Doc had taken out his permanent marker and drawn a curly handlebar mustache on the ensign's face. The guys were adding glasses, devil horns and a goatee.

"Okay, that's enough," Mike ordered, taking the marker. He knew they were just relieving tension. But he wanted to maintain a level of professionalism above reproach on this mission. He gave Nouri a shake but couldn't rouse him. "Let Sleeping Beauty rest. We're going to need him later." Like the marker, the tag Sleeping Beauty wouldn't wear off for a while. "Itch, you'd better radio ahead to the *Enterprise,* see if they have a Marine detachment on board with any snipers. Just in case."

"Mac," Ajax said, "your sister came through. We at least have an itinerary and a crude idea of what the ship looks like from the brochure. The ship's capacity is 1778, with a crew of seven hundred. Eleven decks. Signal, sun, boat, upper, quarter, and one through seven. She said your parents are on the sun deck in stateroom number 8183."

His men stopped to absorb this bit of info.

Mike took the marker and wrote the number across the palm of his hand.

USS ENTERPRISE CVN 65
Somewhere in the South China Sea

THE SEAHAWKS WERE TO TOUCH DOWN, refuel, recharge and take off again shortly after midnight. Meanwhile, Mike was in constant contact with the admiral and the rest of his task force.

"Mac." Itch handed him the SATCOM on the way to the flight deck. "It's the Secretary of the Navy *and* the Secretary of Defense."

That meant his orders were coming directly from the President of the United States. "Yes, sir, Mr. Secretary," Mike said. From somewhere deep inside the Pentagon the two men briefed him from over a speaker phone, which meant he'd be briefing his men en route.

On board the gunship, Mike took the courtesy crash helmet Hannah offered, then tuned out the chatter of her start-up procedures and engine rattle. He spoke into the mouthpiece of the comm he and his men wore and delivered their updated briefing. With the helmet on, Hannah would also be able to hear him.

"Things are getting a little out of hand on the *King Neptune.* The six hijackers are having a hard time keeping the hundred and three passengers and crew under control. They came up with this number by taking a head count of the onshore passengers in Taiwan and comparing it to the passenger and crew lists. There are eleven Americans on board and the President is counting on us to see that nothing happens to them.

"The hijackers are our familiar Tango partners, al-

Ayman. They're demanding the release of Mullah Kahn's two sons from Gitmo, along with a list of other prisoners being held in the U.S. and allied nations.

"You can imagine the President's response to that. But here's our deal. We've got to take these guys in international waters because we have no less than ten countries breathing down our necks on this one. Zero civilian causalities. We go in. We do our job. And we do it clean."

"Mac?" Itch asked. "Did they find out if your parents were on board?"

"Yes, my folks are on board."

HANNAH'S HEART just about stopped when she heard that, but she kept on course at an air speed of one hundred and eighty knots. Shortly after McCaffrey's heart-wrenching pronouncement came the command to "Stand down."

The hijackers had surrendered to the Australian government. Since the cruise liner was registered to Australia, the Aussie equivalent of the SEALs, the SASR—Special Air Services Regiment—got the nod and was heading toward the *King Neptune.*

Mike's and Hannah's teams had been debriefed aboard the USS *Enterprise,* returned to Guam and were now on their way back home on a C-130. Mike hadn't spoken a word to Hannah since their mission was aborted.

The part of the task force in the P.I. had taken down a cargo ship of terrorist weapons that had been on a collision course for a port in Bali to make a statement. If this was any other mission she would have attributed McCaffrey's sullen silence to being left out of the action. But she imagined he had a lot more on his mind right now, like relief, and no way to release it.

"I wonder if your parents will be taking the free cruise they earned anytime soon," she said, trying to break the ice.

"Excuse me." He drained his cup, tossed the empty to the trash and opened the head door. She shoved him inside and locked the door behind them. "What the—"

She slammed the full weight of her body against him, her mouth hot and heavy on his. Panting from the onslaught, he pulled her off by the shoulders. They locked gazes. Just when she thought he was going to shake her, he returned his mouth to hers full force.

She fumbled with his belt. His zipper. His buttons. Heard the rasp of her flight-suit zipper. His hands were everywhere. It was all she could do to hang on. He drove into her hard, demanding. She was wet, responding to his need. Her want.

The C-130's engines roared in her ears and hummed through her body. She bit back his name.

He slumped against her. Then he pulled away. And began to get dressed. "What the hell, Stanton, you had the sudden urge to join the mile-high club?"

"You looked…tense."

"And you're—what? My tension reliever? Thanks, I'm so calm now." The hand he raked through his hair was shaking.

She ignored his bluster and held his hand, then kissed it. "I just thought that since we were gonna go to hell and back together, I'd try and make the return trip a little more enjoyable."

"Together, huh?"

"Get used to it. *Homonoia. Homophrosune.* Oneness of mind and heart. You did say for all eternity."

CHAPTER NINETEEN

NAVAL AMPHIBIOUS BASE
Coronado, California

"WHO'S COMING HOME TODAY?" Mike held Fallon under her arms in the water.

"Fal-lon," she said in her sweet baby singsong.

"No," he said. "Hold your breath." She pursed her little lips. He pulled her under with him. Held her there. Let her go. She kicked toward him through the chlorine blue water. Bubbles escaped her mouth as she smiled, and he brought her to the surface again.

She took a surprised breath.

"Who's coming home today?"

"Dad-dy."

"No." He shook his head. "Daddy's right here."

"Dad-dy," she repeated.

"Momma's coming home today!"

"Dad-dy!" she argued.

"You gotta give me this one, Fallon," he said, carrying her out of the pool. "It's been a long time since we've seen Momma. *Six whole months.* Momma's gonna be so excited to see you." They'd had a good twelve months together as a family before Hannah had deployed. Well, almost a family. Circumstances had kept them from tying the knot, and they weren't officially husband and wife...yet.

"Dad-dy."

It was his fault. He was the parent who'd been lucky enough to spend more time with their daughter. He'd covered some ops in his old stomping grounds, the P.I., but HCS-9 had relieved HCS-5 in Kuwait on a six-month rotation.

He'd forbidden the word Momma, when Fallon started calling her aunt that. He'd shown her Hannah's picture every day. They had the camera phone, baby cam and e-mail. And this past week he and Sammy and Rosemary had T-shirts made with Hannah's picture on them.

Still not a Momma out of Fallon's stubborn little mouth.

Their swim instructor handed them their certificate as they were leaving. He'd only missed two classes in the six-week course, and Samantha had filled in for him.

"Who are we?" he asked.

"Tadpo'es."

"Tadpoles," he agreed with the certificate to prove it. She had a good vocabulary for a two-year-old, just not the one word he was desperate for.

They changed and drove home.

"How was swimming today?" Sammy greeted them, taking Fallon from him. "I'll bet she's hungry. I'll feed her. Then change her."

"Sam-my." Fallon reached for her aunt.

"Graduated top of the Tadpoles," Mike bragged.

"Michael." Rosemary came down the stairs carrying a box. "I found this and you said if I ever found any of Van's things to run them by you. I believe these are the personal effects the Navy delivered. I never could bring myself to open the thing."

"Thank you, Rosemary," he said, kissing her on the cheek. Not because he was in the habit of kissing his soon-to-be mother-in-law. But because he was so happy. He took the box from her and carried it to the kitchen table.

He'd asked Rosemary to move back in temporarily, when Hannah had deployed and he'd moved into Hannah's room. Now that he was there he had no intention of moving out. Fallon was settled across the hall. It was time for Hannah and him to have their nights together, at least until the next time one or both of them deployed.

He broke the seal and lifted the lid.

Rosemary stood by wringing her hands. "Well."

He lifted out a large birthday-wrapped package.

"Oh, my. I'd forgotten," she said. "He always bought his gifts in advance."

Mike knew all about that. It was something he'd always done himself. And before Hannah left, they'd sat down and planned all the birthdays and holidays she'd miss. Including Fallon's second birthday. The other items in the box were things you might find in a guy's locker, things he'd want with him but wouldn't want to take into the field. His wallet. His wedding ring. Pictures of his family.

Rosemary sorted through the items, eyes glistening with tears. It seemed Van had one last letter in there. She tucked it away to read in private later.

"It's almost time," he said, checking his watch.

"Fallon's ready," Sammy announced.

"Do you have the invitations?" Mike asked. "I'll drop them in the mail on the way."

Rosemary handed over the wedding invitations. "Are you sure you know what you're doing?"

"I'm hedging my bet," he said, taking Fallon from her aunt. "Ready to go get Momma, sweet pea?" His daughter wore yellow, and he wore his Hannah T-shirt.

On the way to the base he tried several more times to get Fallon to say Momma.

"Look who's coming," he said, finally spotting her on the tarmac. His chest squeezed so tight he couldn't breathe.

Fallon looked. Cried. Buried her face in his shoulder.

"Oh, Fallon, come on. Not now."

She cried louder.

Hannah spotted them and picked up her pace. He wrapped his arm around her and hugged her close. Tears pricked her eyes. She forced a weak smile for their daughter who wouldn't even look at her.

"Look, Fallon," Mike cajoled. "Momma's home." He tried to pry their daughter from his arms to place her in her mother's.

"Don't," Hannah insisted. "She'll come to me when she's ready." She brushed her daughter's hair. Fallon looked up, still crying, always so mad at Hannah during these reunions. But they saw their chance, and Mike slipped Fallon into Hannah's waiting arms.

Fallon continued to cry. Hannah began to cry. "I know, baby, Momma smells like dirty socks."

Some glimmer of recognition sparked. Fallon looked at her father and then back at her mother. She stopped crying long enough to suck her thumb.

"You're so big! Momma's missed you so much. You don't even remember me, do you? That's okay."

Mike felt about as helpless as Hannah looked.

Fallon rested her head against Hannah's breast. "Mom-ma," she said. The sweetest word Mike had ever heard.

"Momma," Hannah repeated, tears streaming down her face.

"I missed you, Han," he said. "I had something else planned, but I can't wait any longer." He reached into the diaper bag. Encouraged by the light in her eyes, he continued, "I've been carrying this around for a couple of months now, waiting for you to come home. I know you can't wear a ring in the cockpit…" he opened the ring box to show her a simple gold chain and three baby rings, each with their birthstones "…but I thought you might be able to take this along."

He waited for recognition to dawn. Her birthstone was a miniature of her class ring, as was his. It was customary for an officer to give his sweetheart a miniature of his class ring when he proposed.

"I love…it," she said with tears in her eyes.

"Is that a yes?"

"Yes."

"Then you'll need this," he said, digging into his jeans pocket. "Decoder ring, right out of a Cracker Jack box." He slipped the single solitaire on her left ring finger.

Captain and Mrs. Jon Jordan "JJ" Loring
request the honor of your presence
at the marriage of her daughter
Hannah C. Stanton
Lieutenant Commander, United States Navy Reserve
to
Commander Sean Michael "Mac" McCaffrey,
United States Navy
on Saturday, the twenty-second of July
at ten o'clock
Base Chapel, Naval Air Station Fallon
and afterward at the reception
Silver State Officers' Club
Fallon, Nevada

RSVP   Uniform
(619)545-XXXX Service Dress Whites

NAVAL AIR STATION
Fallon, Nevada

HANNAH STEPPED ONTO the white carpet. *Alone.*

In marriage as in life, one should start out as one intended to go along. For Hannah that meant without leaning on any man.

However, just because she didn't need one, didn't mean she didn't want one.

Mike adjusted the collar of his Dress Whites and she smiled. Yeah, she'd bet he was sweating under there. But after the mother of the bride was seated, the lieutenant escorts hooked on their swords and there were enough armed swordsmen in the room to see that the groom wasn't going anywhere.

And when Mike's gaze locked on her, she knew beyond a shadow of a doubt he was here to stay. She was glad she'd chosen to wear the simple sleeveless white gown instead of her uniform, because his eyes lit up the chapel.

She carried a bouquet of white and champagne roses.

Syd, Meg and Sammy, in their champagne bridesmaids' dresses all preceded her up the aisle. She was glad to see that her old college roommate had made it to the wedding, as well as Peter.

Fallon followed Sammy, dropping her rose petals, then stopping and bending over to pick them up, even as Sammy urged her forward.

When Fallon saw her daddy, she dropped her basket and ran to him. He picked her up and Hannah met them at the altar.

Everything else was just a blur. Until it came time to kiss the bride. Then the day was just perfect.

They'd done it. They'd actually done it!

Following their trip back up the aisle, and family-filled photo opportunities, came the Arch of Swords. The chapel door opened with his lieutenants on one side, hers on the other. Even Spence. All gleaming white in their Service Dress best.

"Officers, draw swords." The command was given by Mike's Executive Officer. The swords were drawn from their scabbards in one continuous motion, each rising to touch the tip of the opposite sword. "Invert swords." A quick turn of the wrist so that the cutting edge was up.

"Ready?" Mike asked, taking her hand while holding Fallon in the other arm.

"How fast can you run?" Hannah asked.

"Oh, no, you're not getting out of this one. It's tradition," he teased. They ran down the chapel steps and through the Arch of Swords to the cheers of their bird-seed-throwing family and friends.

The last swordsman in line, Mike's XO, whacked her on the butt. "Welcome to the Navy, Mrs. McCaffrey." Hannah paused long enough to glare at Ajax, and he popped to attention. Saluted with his sword. "I mean, welcome to the Navy, Lieutenant Commander McCaffrey, ma'am!"

She'd agreed to marry Mike only after her two years of active duty service were up. She was, of course, still a weekend warrior, ready and waiting for the call to serve. And she'd have plenty of time *after* the honeymoon to decide her next career move.

She could go back to work for Hall-Petrone, but she thought maybe, for the next couple of years anyway, weekend warrior/stay-at-home mom sounded just about right. The dream was for more babies and for Mike to retire young enough to enjoy them. But for now, living in the moment was enough.

Mike handed Fallon over to his mom outside the waiting limo. Fallon would be staying with her cousins for the duration of the honeymoon.

Hannah crawled into the back seat, and Mike climbed in beside her. Maybe they'd drive to Grime's Point before heading to the reception, which was right across the street.

There was a birthday present on the seat across from them, torn and faded with age. "Wedding present," he said somberly. "Your father wanted to be here and couldn't."

"Don't make me cry on my wedding day." She didn't make a move to pick it up. Instead she clung to his hand.

"Aren't you going to open it?"

"I already know what it is," she said. "I think I'd like to save it for Fallon. Maybe for her seventh birthday."

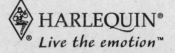

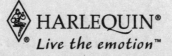

Harlequin Romance®

A compelling miniseries from Harlequin Romance

From paper marriage...to wedded bliss?

A wedding dilemma:

What should a sexy, successful bachelor do if he's too busy making millions to find a wife, or finds the perfect woman and just has to strike a bridal bargain...?

The perfect proposal:

The solution? For better, for worse, these grooms in a hurry have decided to sign, seal and deliver the ultimate marriage contract...to buy a bride!

Don't miss the latest CONTRACT BRIDES story coming next month by emotional author Barbara McMahon.

Her captivating style and believable characters will leave your romance senses tingling!

September—Marriage in Name Only (HR #3813)

Starting in September,
Harlequin Romance has a fresh new look!

Available wherever Harlequin books are sold.

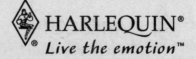

www.eHarlequin.com

HRBMMINO

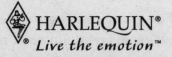